INTRODUCTION

SOME years ago Mr. Read published an account of his childhood under the title *The Innocent Eye*. It must have come as a surprise to many of his readers that the author of *Art Now* was brought up on a Yorkshire farm: a whole world of the imagination seems to separate the rather dry sophisticated critic from the vale, the orchard, the foldgarth, the mill and the stockyard—the fine simple stony architecture of his childhood.

'The basin at times was very wide, especially in the clearness of a summer's day; but as dusk fell it would suddenly contract, the misty hills would draw near, and with night they had clasped us close. the centre of the world had become a candle shining from the kitchen window. Inside, in the sitting-room where we spent most of our life, a lamp was lit, with a ground glass shade like a full yellow moon. There we were bathed from the fire, said our prayers kneeling on the hearthrug, and then disappeared up the steep stairs lighted by a candle to bed.'

Later, in *Annals of Innocence and Experience*, Mr. Read took the account of his own life on out of the Yorkshire vale; a grim Spartan orphans' school with a strong religious tone and the young Read absorbed in Rider Haggard; a clerkship in a Leeds Savings Bank at £20 a year, and the slightly older Read becoming a Tory and reading Disraeli and Burke; then Leeds University and loss of faith, religious and political, and so the war, and after it the literary career—and the settled literary personality, the agnostic, the anarchist and the romantic.

v

We should never have known without *The Innocent Eye* quite how far Mr. Read had travelled. That is the astounding thing—Mr. Read was able to go back, back from the intellectual atmosphere personified in Freud, Bergson, Croce, Dewey, Vivant, Scheler. . . . And if we examine his work there have always been phases when he has returned; the creative spirit has been more than usually separated in his case from the critical mind. (He admits himself in one essay that submitting to the creative impulse he has written poetry which owes nothing to his critical theories.) The critic, one feels, has sometimes been at pains to adopt the latest psychological theories before they have proved their validity, but the creative spirit has remained tied to innocence. 'The only real experiences in life,' writes Mr. Read, 'being those lived with a virgin sensibility—so that we only hear a tone once, only see a colour once, see, hear, touch, taste and smell everything but once, the first time.'

The mill where Olivero rescues the Green Child Siloën from the sullen bullying passion of Kneeshaw is Read's uncle's mill—just as the stream which the returning traveller finds has reversed its course is 'the mysterious water' of *The Innocent Eye* which dived underground and re-emerged in the same uncle's field. And it may not be too imaginative to trace the dreadful sight that met Olivero's eyes through the mill window as Kneeshaw tried to force the Green Child to drink the blood of a newly killed lamb to that occasion in the foldgarth when the child Read caught his finger in the machine for crushing oil-cake. 'I fainted with the pain, and the horror of that dim milk-white panic is as ineffaceable as the scar which my flesh still bears.'

'Milk-white panic': like the Green Child herself, Mr. Read has a horror of violence. The conflict always

The Green Child

by

Herbert Read

Introduction by
Graham Greene

Robin Clark
London

First published in paperback by Robin Clark Ltd. in 1989
27/29 Goodge Street
London W1P 1FD

First published by William Heineman Ltd. 1935

British Library Cataloguing in Publication Data
Read, Herbert 1893–1968
The Green Child.
I. Title
823'.912 [F]
ISBN 0-86072-122-1

Printed and bound in Great Britain by
Cox & Wyman Ltd, Reading, Berks

present in his work is between the fear and the glory—
between the 'milk-white panic' and the vision which was
felt by 'the solitary little alien in the streets of Leeds,'
the uncontrollable ambition which 'threw into the
cloudy future an infinite ray in which there could always
be seen, like a silver knight on a white steed, this unreal
figure which was myself, riding to quixotic combats,
attaining a blinding and indefinable glory.' If art is
always the resolution of a combat, here is surely the
source of Mr. Read's finest work.

Glory, it must be remembered, is not merely martial
glory, or ambition. 'Glory is the radiance in which virtues flourish. The love of glory is the sanction of great
deeds: all greatness and magnanimity proceed not from
calculation but from an instinctive desire for the quality
of glory. Glory is distinguished from fortune, because
fortune exacts care; you must connive with your fellows
and compromise yourself in a thousand ways to make
sure of its fickle favours. Glory is gained directly, if one
has the genius to deserve it: glory is sudden.'

In his novel *The Green Child* Mr. Read conveyed, as
he had never done before, that private sense of glory.
We see it working inwards from political glory—the
ideal state which Olivero founded in South America and
found so unsatisfying ('try as I would I could not solve
my personal problem in social terms')—back to the real
source of inspiration, the home of the 'innocent eye,' the
dream of complete 'sudden' glory—the absolute surrender of self. Alone in his crystalline grotto, in the mysterious unpolitical country, somewhere below the earth's
surface, to which the Green Child had led him, sinking
through the water at the mill-stream's source, the former
dictator awaits death and petrification—the sense of sin,
passion, the fear of death, all the motives of conflict

which could not be excluded from his republic or from the human heart have been eliminated. Desire is limited to the desire of the final surrender, of becoming first rock, then crystal, of reaching permanency like an image —the pursuit of glory could hardly go further.

'When the hated breath at last left the human body, that body was carried to special caves, and then laid in troughs filled with the petrous water that dripped from roof and walls. There it remained until the body turned white and hard, until the eyes were glazed under the vitreous lids, and the hair of the head became like crisp snail-shells, the beard like a few jagged icicles. . . .'

It is the same sense of glory that impelled Christian writers to picture the City of God—both are fantasies, both are expressions of a dream unattainable by the author. The difference, of course, is that the Christian artist believed that his fantasy was somewhere attainable: the agnostic knows that no Green Child will ever really show him the way to absolute glory. The difference—though for the living suffering man it represents all the difference between hell and purgatory—is not to us important. Christian faith might have borne poorer fruits than this sense of unattainable glory lodged in the child's brain on a Yorkshire farm forty years ago.

GRAHAM GREENE.

March, 1946.

1

THE assassination of President Olivero, which took place in the autumn of 1861, was for the world at large one of those innumerable incidents of a violent nature which characterise the politics of the South American continent. For twenty-four hours it loomed large in the headlines of the newspapers; but beyond an intimation, the next day, that General Iturbide had formed a provisional government with the full approval of the military party, the event had no further reverberations in the outer world. President Olivero, who had arranged his own assassination, made his way in a leisurely fashion to Europe. On the way he allowed his beard to grow.

When he disembarked in Spain, he seemed unremarkable enough, for the return of the emigrant, swarthy and bearded from a life on the pampas, was a common event in that country. But Spain was not where he designed to stay; for though the Spanish language had become natural to him, so that he habitually used it in thought and speech, his real nationality was English, and the ruling desire in all his present conduct was to return to his native land and particularly to the scenes of his childhood. Thirty years had elapsed since his precipitate departure—thirty long years during which those scenes had withdrawn to a fantastic distance, bright and exquisite and miniature, like a landscape seen through the wrong end of a telescope. But though the sentimental nostalgia which consumed his being was so strong, his rational fear of disillusionment was also considerable, and it was only with many haltings and invented delays that he approached England. In Spain, in Provence, in Switzerland, in Paris—wherever he stopped on his slow progress northwards—he lingered to test his sense of reality. Reality? That may not be the right word to describe the contrast between two states of mind, one of which is drinking in the bright charm of tangible things, of picturesque towns and people, of hill and sky, of food and wine, of books and papers casually bought, of music overheard; the other occupied by a landscape distant and withdrawn in the long dark tunnel of time, but bright in its crystal setting. He who had practised so successfully the art of forgetting, now sought to revive in himself the art of remembering. He found that the first essential was to resign all conscious attempts at recalling the past. Events and places in their individuality demand a place in time, and after thirty years, how can one reconstitute a sense of time? To escape from the sense of time, to live in the eternity of what he was accustomed to call "the divine essence of things"—that was his only desire. But it was this very essence that now impelled him to return to the place where his personality had first been liberated, in circumstances extraordinary enough to make them the enduring reality of his life.

Once in England he no longer delayed, but made straight for his native village. He had left it on foot, and had walked nearly forty miles to the nearest railway; but now a new line carried him to the village itself. From a junction on the main line, the train took a meandering course among the hills, stopping at every station and sometimes waiting for a considerable time to allow cattle or goods to be loaded. Olivero—in England his name had been Oliver—still retained the black cloak and wide-brimmed hat in which he had left South America, and he was therefore a conspicuous figure among the country farmers and their wives who, from time to time, shared the carriage with him. He remained silent and reserved in his corner, gazing out on the countryside and noticing the signs of change which thirty years had inevitably produced. Late in the afternoon he found himself in familiar country: the outline of the hills, the wooded slopes, the church towers and an isolated house or two were recognised with an unexpected access of emotion; but the towns, with their stations and accompanying sheds, were seen from a strange aspect. He was relieved to find that his own station was some distance from the village: he was not prepared to plunge too suddenly into the heart of his past. He left his bag at the station, and waited until the last of the passengers who had descended with him had disappeared down the lane which led to the village. Then he followed them slowly, his head bent, as if afraid that to look up and around would disturb him too much. When he reached the first houses it was nearly dusk.

The village consisted of two streets, crossing at the market-place. A stream ran along the road he was taking, with houses beyond it, approached sometimes by only a broad plank, sometimes by a wooden bridge with hand-rails, and in a few cases by a stone culvert. When it reached the market-place the river bent round to the right, still accompanying the road which went in that direction. Here it was separated from the road by a line of sycamore trees, and the prospect, as one looked along the street, with the old almshouses on one side, the sycamores and the river with the high wall of the Hall beyond it on the other side, was one of the prettiest in England. Beyond noticing that the trees were bigger and the shade denser than he had remembered, Olivero looked neither to the right nor the left, but made straight across the market-place to the inn, where he found a room and arranged to have his bag brought from the station.

These preliminaries settled, he came out into the market-place again, and sat for a moment on a bench by the market cross. Lights were beginning to appear in the cottage windows, but except for an occasional figure going from house to house, there was scarcely anyone about. He sat listening to intimate sounds—voices in the soft dialect he had once spoken, the click of a raised latch, the rattle of a milk-pail, the chiming of clocks in the houses; and underneath all these occasional sounds, the persistent lapping of the stream in its pebbly bed. A white railing opposite him ran along the edge of the stream, and presently he got up and went across to this railing, and leant against it as he gazed down into the rippling water.

It was then that he noticed, or thought he noticed, an extraordinary fact. The stream as he remembered it— and he could remember the pressure of its current against his bare legs as he waded among its smooth flat pebbles —ran in the direction of the station from which he had just come. But now, indubitably, it was flowing in the opposite direction, towards the church. The reflection of the moon, which had now risen placidly above the syca- mores, made this clear in the fluctuating ripple of the stream; whilst here and there a stone projecting above the surface curled the water back against the force of the current. For something like an hour Olivero remained as if transfixed to the white railing; for the whole structure of his memory was challenged. He recalled detail after detail of his early experience in relation to the stream : the trout suspended with their heads upstream which he had often observed from the stone bridge by the church

—it had been one of his favourite amusements to try and drop a stone on the unsuspecting fish, but of course the fish always shot away before ever the stone had touched the surface of the water; the pool below the mill where they used to bathe—and here he distinctly remembered the sagging branches of the willows with long beards of faded weed, and how—yes, positively—these wisps when caught by the bank of the stream inclined towards the village; besides, the mill itself was a mile's distance upstream, beyond the church, and beyond the mill the stream made its way—which is a manner of speaking, because it had made its way in the opposite direction—made its way through the meadows and the woods until it came to the open fells, and there, among the slopes, it had its source. He had often followed the bed of the stream on a long day's excursion right up to this source, a bog scented with low bushes of myrtle and bright with yellow-green patches of butterwort. There could be no doubt that the stream rose out yonder beyond the church and flowed through the village in the direction of the railway-station. But yet—unless his eyes deceived him—there before him was positive evidence that the stream now flowed in the opposite direction, towards the church.

His first impulse was to seek for some physical explanation of the phenomenon he had observed. The meanderings of a stream, for example, can be very deceptive. All kinds of obstacles divert the natural flow of water towards the lower level of the sea—inequalities in the height and hardness of the ground, not to mention the deliberate interference of man—so that a stream which is flowing from the north to the south at one point can easily be flowing from the south to the north at another point not so far away. Ask any man in what direction he would be travelling when he passes through the Panama Canal from the Atlantic to the Pacific Ocean, and if he deigned to answer at all he would say, most often, from east to west; or if he suspected a catch, he might say, from north to south; he would never suspect the truth, which is that owing to the contortions of that strange isthmus, his actual direction would be from west to east. It is not to be expected, therefore, that a stream should always keep to the same direction in its progress towards the sea: in reality it may move through all the points of the compass. But from where Olivero stood in the market-place, to the bridge near the church where he had watched the trout, the stream ran straight; there was no possibility of a deflecting meander. He came to the conclusion, therefore, that the direction of the stream, if changed it had been, must have been changed by human agency—he dismissed, incidentally, the thought that did for a moment flash through his brain, that possibly an earthquake had shifted the levels of the land in some way and so caused a contrary flow; for earthquakes, of course, never occur in England.

He decided, late as it was, to proceed upstream to solve the problem. The moonlight was sufficiently strong to show the way, and who knows but that in the dark his early instincts might the easier revive and reveal to him the paths which he had known as a boy—fishermen's paths along the banks of the stream, difficult paths for any stranger. But before actually setting out, he bent over the stream by a stone step where the villagers brought their pails to fill, and drawing back his cloak and sleeve, he dipped his hand in the stream, right up to his sensitive wrist, and felt the flow of the cold water, thus confirming by an independent sense the impression which he had received from his eyes. While like most men he was content to be guided by the superior sense of sight, yet there was no harm—indeed, some considerable comfort—in adding yet another sensual witness to such a rationally incomprehensible fact.

It was now about eight o'clock. He had had tea at the junction where he had changed for the branch line, and in this part of the country tea is the last meal of the day. There was no reason, therefore, why he should return to the inn, and the innkeeper might naturally suppose that he had gone out to visit friends. The main street was now quite deserted—in an hour most of the lights would be out, for already people were going to bed. He walked slowly along until he came to the stone bridge; here the street went straight on, whilst the stream, still accompanied by a smaller road, turned to the left. There was not much point in lingering on the bridge: it arched itself high above the bed of the stream, and at night there were no fish to be seen. But as if only to repeat an earlier habit, Olivero went and looked over the stone cresting, down to where the water looked black and sullen in the shadow of the arch. Nothing, however, was to be gained by staying there, and he soon left the bridge and took the road to the mill.

There was still no perceptible incline in the ground, so Olivero did not stop to consider whether there was yet a contradiction in that elementary law of physics which decrees that water can never flow uphill. That law, as he now recalled, Olivero had had some difficulty in believing when it was first enunciated to him at school. He knew long stretches of the stream, which when seen from a neighbouring hill, had all the appearance of sloping upwards in the direction of the flow. Besides, water was not a powerless element; it had cohesion, as you might observe in a drop of rain, clinging like a crystal bead to the edge of a cabbage-leaf, mirroring the whole world on its hard surface. Again, it had always seemed possible to his boyish reasoning that the force which impelled water downwards should be capable of impelling the same water upwards—and when it was explained to him that this force was the force of gravity, it still seemed a reasonable calculation to allow that a stream of water which had fallen for x number of feet over a distance of y miles, should be capable of rising $x-n$ number of feet over a distance of $y-n^1$ miles. The factor n might, of course, be considerable, owing to the regrettable tendency of water to slip backwards; but still, on any reasonable basis of probability, one might expect a stream to flow up a gentle incline of say five hundred yards.

He remembered these childish calculations as he proceeded along the road to the mill. He was now on exceedingly familiar ground—so familiar that years ago he had known the colour and shape of every stone embedded in the footpath, every variation in the shape and composition of the hedge which presently bordered the right side of the road, now that the last cottages were passed. For the greater part of his childhood the mill had been his home, and this path he had taken daily between the house and the school. The other side of the stream was here bordered by a high hedge of ragged trees—elderberry, willow, ash and blackthorn; under their overhanging branches the water-hens used to dart in and out. Soon he could see the long white front of the mill shining in the moonlight, and to the right, half buried in a huge copper-beech tree, the mill-house. But as he approached he became aware, with a trepidation he could not justify, of changes—changes in the atmosphere, the sound of the water, the vague outline of trees and hedges. His pace grew slower and he finally stopped, to try and assess, in the moonlight, the evidences of the changes confronting him. He stood at a point where, in former days, there should have been a shallow ford in front of him and a footbridge to the right; for at this point the river divided into a loop, one arm, the one on his left as he stood, being the water which had passed through the mill from the dam beyond, the other, on the right, being the natural course of the stream. But the ford and the white footbridge had now disappeared, and the road to the mill ran fair and level over a brick culvert. Advancing slowly to this new bridge, he discovered an unexpected flow of water beneath him; but this phenomenon was explained almost at once by his further discovery that the water which had formerly flowed in rather noisy force from the diverted mill-race, had now entirely ceased, the bed of this side of the loop being quite overgrown with grasses and willow-herb. This surely implied that the mill had ceased to function, or perhaps was now run by some power other than water. But the blank deserted look of everything, even in the moonlight, pointed all too surely to the former explanation, and when Olivero approaching nearer, this explanation was confirmed by the broken unglazed windows, in which one or two old sacks flapped desolately. There was no light in the house itself, but the garden was tidy and a cat sprang from the acacia tree by the garden-gate and came to rub its sleek body against his leg.

Olivero returned to the stream. He was now quite certain that his memory had not deceived him, and that the direction of the current had actually changed. The reason was still to seek. He recrossed the culvert and took the path which led round to the back of the mill, to the dam and the weir. Here little had changed, but the supporting bank between the weir and the dam had

been partially washed away or destroyed, thus allowing
the stream to resume its natural direction, along a bed
which he remembered as the beginning of a cart-track
leading from the mill to a disused tannery half a mile
upstream. Intent on solving his mystery, he pursued his
way along the side of the stream, stumbling for a time
through a rank growth of nettles and hemlock, but
eventually gaining the ruins of the tannery, where once
more he was on familiar ground. A clearly-defined path
now led along the side of the stream; on his right was a
wood, but over the stream were the meadows which belonged to the mill, and beyond them, parallel to the
stream, would be the road which led to the moors. For a
few moments he deliberated: it was getting late and he
was uncertain how long the moonlight would last. He
might perhaps cross the stream and make across the
meadows for the road, which rejoined the stream two
miles farther up the valley: the going would be easier in
the dark, and surely there could be no intervening cause
to explain the stream's change of direction. But the
events of the last hour, especially the discovery of the
deserted mill, had so thoroughly imbued him with a
sense of uncertainty, that he determined to take no
chances, and with an occasional glance at the stream,
made his way as quickly as he could along the difficult
path before him.

Nothing occurred to interrupt his progress—the stream
flowed on before him; he could both see and hear the
direction of the water. It went laughing over the stones
in its bed, mocking him, luring him onwards. Then
suddenly he perceived lights in front of him, and he
reckoned that they must come from a house known as
the Cauldron, which stood at the point where the moorland road from the village crossed the stream. He re-

membered, with a sudden intuition of the possible explanation of the deserted mill, that the Cauldron too had been a mill of a sort—a small affair with a couple of rough millstones suitable for grinding rough grain, such as rye, into meal for cattle—a mill used by the few outlying moorland farmers to save them the extra cartage involved in bringing their grain to the village. What if this mill had expanded, grown grander and more efficient, until it had finally superseded the village mill? There was no knowing what an ambitious man might do, once the possibility had come into his mind—for power, the only necessary means, was at hand. He remembered, about the time he left the village, some talk of modern machinery that could grind flour finer and whiter than any ever produced before. It was likely enough that the miller at the Cauldron had stolen a march on his conservative rival, installed the new plant and gained all the trade.

As he drew nearer, his supposition was confirmed by the discovery that the several lights in front of him belonged to one building, or group of buildings, and when nearer still he heard the steady hum of machinery. The mill, rebuilt and enlarged, was working through the night. He saw now the flicker of wheels and the flurry of straps through an open window. The path brought him up against a garden fence, and he realised that he would have to make his way through the mill-yard, past the house. He was a little loth to do this, for fear of being stopped and questioned—not that he had a guilty conscience about the investigation he was making, but still, it would be difficult to explain his business to people who might not see the importance it had for him, who might even consider him a little mad, wandering about at midnight on such an apparently unimportant errand. Instead, therefore, of passing through the yard gate, he made his way round the back of the house, on the side overlooking the fields, intending to rejoin the stream beyond the mill.

At this side of the house a single window threw its bright light across the field—an open window on the ground floor, quite near to the level of the ground. Olivero's instinct was to avoid the fan of light by making a wide detour in the field, but he was deflected from this intention by the unexpected appearance of a figure, that of a man, who loomed out of the darkness beyond the light, carrying a burden in his arms. As this figure drew nearer the light, the burden was clearly to be recognised as a lamb, quite still and perhaps dead, which the man proceeded to pass through the open window, and then to follow himself, first thrusting in his legs, and turning to draw his body after them, for the window was low and inconvenient. The whole procedure took place with the quickness and certainty of an act deliberately done, and naturally aroused the curiosity of the unsuspected onlooker. Olivero realised that at the time of year it was perhaps not unusual for a lamb to die of exposure, but the weather was exceptionally fine; and why, in any case, should the lamb be rescued at midnight, and taken into the house with such obvious secrecy? It occurred to him, that as most people have a repugnance for the flesh of animals that have died naturally (that is to say, from the act of God, and not in a slaughter-house), and as most cattle-owners resent the loss incurred in this way, the man might be smuggling in the dead animal to pass it off, later, as a slaughtered one. But the lamb appeared to be too small for the table, and in such a lonely place it would not be difficult to do the smuggling by light of day. Some other explanation seemed necessary, and for the moment the problem of the stream ceased to pre-occupy his mind.

He stood for a few minutes in the shadow of the wall and then began to sidle slowly towards the light. He was perhaps ten feet away when he drew up petrified by a shrill scream that issued from the open window. But his rigidity only lasted a second; he darted to the window, and acting now instinctively, fell flat on the ground and slowly raised his head to the level of the sill. There once again he was held transfixed.

On a bare table to the right lay the lamb; its throat had been cut and was bleeding into a large bowl, over the edge of which its head hung pathetically. In the middle of the room the man stood, drawing back the head of a woman by the hair and compelling her to drink from a cup which he held in his hand. So much was clear at a glance; then Olivero noticed that the woman, who was extraordinarily frail and pallid, was bound by a rope to the chair in which she was seated, and that her expression was one of concentrated terror as she struggled to refuse the proffered cup. The blood which she was being forced to drink dribbled down each side of her mouth and fell in bright stains down the front of her white dress. The light came from a paraffin lamp, whose golden globe swung impassively above this scene of terror.

In such circumstances a man does not act consciously; he is suddenly presented with a situation to which he cannot be a passive onlooker, but in which he must partici-pate. Strange fluids pass into his blood-stream, his eyes dilate, his hair bristles on his scalp, his nostrils distend. For thirty years, much against his natural inclinations, Olivero had been a man of action. On many occasions he had been compelled to act violently and suddenly, and though after the event it was invariably difficult for him to reconstruct the timeless elements of his actions, and impossible to explain to himself their motivation, yet he had always acquitted himself well—gaining without conscious effort a reputation for courage and even for reckless bravado little in consonance with the ordinary mood of his existence. And so now, without hesitation, he hurled himself into the room, legs foremost as he had observed the man do; but, unfortunately, as he clung to the sash of the window to raise himself and twist his body round, the sash descended and left him in an incongruous position, the upper half of his body outside the window, his legs waving wildly inside the room. This mishap, which in any normal circumstances would have been merely comic, gave a still further fantastic turn to the scene of horror inside the room, but it also served to dispel the instinctive defences which a man might be expected to put up when suddenly confronted by the complete figure of an opponent. As it was, the man in the room, when he turned and saw the waving legs, merely put the cup he was holding on the table, releasing at the same time the head of the woman. He stood nonplussed whilst Olivero quickly regained his balance, struggled to lift the sash imprisoning him, and finally emerged, hatless and ruffled, but impressive and massive against the low frame of the window.

For a moment the two men remained confronting each other in silence.

Olivero was completely shaken out of the instinctive mode of action. His thoughts raced quickly through his brain. He knew that properly he ought to cry: 'Release that woman,' or words to that effect. The woman, meanwhile, had dropped her head on her breast, softly moaning to herself, not even curious to follow the drama taking place before her. Perhaps it was something in her attitude or appearance which made Olivero realise that anything conventionally dramatic or violent would be useless in the present situation. So making a gesture altogether Spanish in its politeness, he merely said: 'Perhaps I can help?'

The man did not reply, but retreated behind the chair in which the woman was tied. From this point of vantage he continued to eye the intruder with wild but helpless animosity. Keeping his gaze fixed on the man, Olivero advanced into the room a step or two, and in this very act he perceived that his opponent was cowed, and would retreat rather than offer any opposition. Olivero therefore, but still slowly, advanced farther into the room, until close by the woman, and then quietly began to unloosen the cords which bound her.

She remained limp and passive. Her released arms fell like pendulums on each side of the chair; her head re-mained sunk on her breast. Feeling infinitely tender towards such a helpless victim of man's malice, Olivero lifted one arm and began to chafe the bruised wrist. It was then that he noticed a peculiarity in her flesh which explained her strange pallor. The skin was not white, but a faint green shade, the colour of a duck's egg. It was, moreover, an unusually transparent tegument, and through its pallor the branches of her veins and arteries spread, not blue and scarlet, but vivid green and golden. The nails were pale blue, very like a blackbird's eggshell. The faint emanation of odour from her flesh was sweet and a little heavy, like the scent of violets.

Olivero looked up at the man, who stood glowering against the wall. 'It is the Green Child!' he cried. The man merely stared fixedly, but Olivero knew that his guess was right.

For as he chafed the chill wrist, his mind carried him back to that strange event which had caused a sensation, not only in the village, but throughout the whole world of newspapers, the very day he had left home thirty years ago. The news had overtaken him as he pursued his way, and had for long days filled his mind with a sense of wonder, even with a sort of rage that he should no longer be capable of investigating the phenomenon on the spot—he who, in the whole village, would have been the natural person to take charge of such an affair.

Anyone who cares to look up the records will discover that in a certain year—the curious may deduce from what has already been said that it was about the year 1830, but for reasons which will be obvious when this narrative has been read, it was necessary to disguise the time and place of these events—well, in a certain year there appeared in the village of —— in the county of —— two children, apparently about four years old, who could not speak any known language, or explain their origin, or relate themselves in any way to the district—indeed, even the world—in which they were found. Moreover, these children, who were lightly clothed in a green web-like material of obscure manufacture, were further distinguished by the extraordinary quality of their flesh, which was of a green, semi-translucent texture, perhaps more like the flesh of a cactus plant than anything else, but of course much more delicate and sensitive. These children were adopted by a widow woman in the village, in order that they might be educated and civilised—though for that matter they were gentle enough in their manners, indeed timid as fallow deer; but they had no notions of God or of even such morality as an English child of that age has usually acquired. Now, Olivero had never forgotten this strange event—in his mind it had the significance of an un-resolved symbol, obscurely connected with his departure, and connected, too, with the inevitability of his return.

It is not therefore surprising that he should have jumped so quickly to the explanation of the strange appearance of the woman before him. No sooner had he realised her identity than a new state of calmness descended on him. His mind was still extremely active, images of a diverse nature emerging and sinking in rapid succession; but this mental activity resembled the con-tained and poised revolutions of a gyroscope, resting, at one point, in his brain, but otherwise distant, and un-related to the cool element of his flesh.

With his handkerchief he wiped away the traces of blood on the woman's face and then folded her arms across her lap. She was breathing gently, without agita-tion; her eyes had opened, but her fixed gaze was directed to the floor. Olivero looked towards her companion, whose attitude had become less tense and defensive. His head was now turned slightly aside, and something in the sly side-long glance with which he observed Olivero, struck the latter with a sudden sense of recognition.

'You are Kneeshaw,' he said, and then went towards him.

The only effect of this recognition was to deepen the man's fear. To the physical reaction was now added a sense of the mysterious divination possessed by the stranger. But now his fear so possessed him that his body became limp and powerless, and with a moan he fell down at Olivero's feet.

It was far from Olivero's intention to do the man any harm. He was afraid of the feeling of contempt which threatened to possess him; moreover he was now so anxious to solve the mystery of the scene he had witnessed, and so convinced of the special destiny which had brought him to this place and to these people, that he knew he must at any cost restore a relation of confidence. He bent down and took the man by the arm, raised him and led him into a chair at the end of the table. He then went and seated himself at the other end of the table. But he had no sooner done this than he observed the lamb on the dish between them, and felt embarrassed by its presence. So he picked it up and carried it across to the window, and there deposited it outside on the ground, closing the window afterwards. He then returned to the table.

'Kneeshaw,' he began, 'carry your mind back thirty years. You were a schoolboy. Your last days at school— do you remember them? Do you remember one day, one afternoon, your master had spread on the schoolroom table a model railway with a clockwork engine. It was a great novelty in those days—not the kind of toy which now can be bought in any toyshop, but a miniature train carefully constructed by an engineer. That engineer was my uncle, one of the first great railway engineers. He gave me this model railway when I was a boy. Because I had certain ideas about the inadequacy of knowledge—I still remain faithful to them—I was in the habit of allowing you boys to play—to become absorbed in your phantasy and imagination. Whilst you played I watched you, and learnt much about the nature of your minds. Sometimes I watched you unobserved, and on one occasion I saw a boy, whose character was in general sullen and unimpressive, seize the engine and begin winding it up with an evil intensity. You had all been warned not to overwind the engine. This boy suddenly decided to disobey this instruction—to destroy this ingenious toy which he knew was valued by the master and a source of endless delight to his companions. I saw him wind the spring swiftly and strongly, exerting all his strength as the spring grew tight. Then, of course, it snapped; the released coil of metal unrolled and the engine fell from the boy's hand and lay on the table like a disembowelled animal. You, Kneeshaw, were that boy, and I was the master. When that spring snapped, something snapped in my mind. I left the village the next day, and until this day now, thirty years later, I have never returned.'

Kneeshaw sat very still whilst Olivero spoke. His gaze lifted sharply when Olivero revealed his identity, but the feeling that had been roused in him was one of curiosity rather than of amazement. Those past events which had so much significance for Olivero, controlling his personality for years by their steady persistence in his mind, were evoked from the forgotten records of Kneeshaw's past only by the accident of this meeting. The young schoolmaster who had struggled for two years with an intractable group of seven or eight boys had passed entirely out of Kneeshaw's life before he had reached the age of twelve. Kneeshaw remembered him as tall and dark, his face very pale beneath his lank hair. He remembered the classroom—the round table at which they all sat, the black marble mantelpiece with an arm-chair before the fire from which Olivero did most of his teaching—recitation, dictation, spelling and a little arithmetic. The house was still standing—the schoolroom was now the office of Mr. Coverdale, the solicitor, and the first floor was used by the Conservative Club—an ugly town house, out of character with the rest of the village. It stood much farther back from the street than the rest of the houses, and what had once been a garden was now a dreary paved yard, Mr. Coverdale's brass plate being the only bright thing in it. It was as though the village, so harmonious and beautiful in itself, had refused to associate with this hard square block, had pushed it into the background to dilapidate and decay.

The school had come to a sudden end, and the master had left the village; his father at the mill died a few years later and there had been no one left—why should Kneeshaw have remembered anything about him? He remembered the toy engine, but he did not remember his own act of vandalism; he had never known that it had had any connection with Mr. Oliver's sudden departure.

The schoolmaster was speaking again: 'It was a little thing, but it broke a tension in me. My mother was dead; I disliked my father. I had never planned to spend my life as a village schoolmaster, a calling for which I had neither the physical nor the mental aptitude. I thought I might become a poet, but my poetry was gloomy and obscure, and nobody would publish it. I felt impotent and defeated, and longed for external circumstances to force action upon me. I struggled feebly with the ignorance and stupidity of you and your companions, but as I had no faith in knowledge, my only desire was to leave you in possession of innocence and happiness. This was interpreted as weakness or laziness, and gradually parents took away their children, till only a handful was left, a handful of neglected children, the children of parents who did not place any value on education, but merely wished to be rid of an inconvenient burden for a few hours every day. Some of these boys I loved—they were like young animals, like calves or foals, with clumsy limbs and bright eyes and sudden senseless movements. I thought they were without evil until the day I watched you playing with the engine, until the day a spring snapped and the tension was ended. I left you all.'

30

The woman moaned softly in her chair. Olivero looked into her face. She was breathing softly, and seemed near to sleep.

'Tell me about her,' Olivero cried, turning once more towards Kneeshaw, 'the Green Child.'

'The Green Child.' Kneeshaw repeated the words in a low voice. He spoke the words and remained gazing at Olivero. There was nothing in the circumstances to make contact easy between the two men. For fifteen years, since the day he brought the Green Child to this mill as his wife, Kneeshaw had lived a life of isolation. He was unread and almost inarticulate, facing the problems of life with direct instincts, acting from day to day as these instincts dictated. He was now faced by a man who obviously belonged to another world—a world of easy speech, of ideas and sentiments, of complicated experience. There was no natural impulse to communicate with such a man. But tragedy drives us beyond natural behaviour, on to a level where imagination and phantasy rule.

'The Green Child,' he said, 'came to me fifteen years ago.'

'There were two,' said Olivero.

'One died,' replied Kneeshaw. 'He did not live more than a few months in this world. He would not eat—he wasted away. And now this one is tired of this world, and wants to go back to the world they came from.'

'And that is why you were forcing her to drink blood?'

'Yes. For many weeks now she has eaten nothing solid—she drinks water and milk, but even milk she does not willingly take. She is wasting away and will die, because she never eats meat, and has no desire to live.'

'Tell me all. I have heard nothing since the day I left the village.'

31

Kneeshaw then told the story of The Green Children, told it disjointedly and with many interruptions and cross-questionings from Olivero. Meanwhile the Green Child herself had fallen into an unconscious state which might be sleep, for she breathed deeply and regularly.

Kneeshaw told how two strange children had one day appeared walking towards the village from the direction of the moors. He repeated some of the facts about their appearance and behaviour which Olivero already knew, and went on to relate how the woman who had first seen them, old Mrs. Hardie who had once been Olivero's nurse, had taken the children into her cottage, and clothed them and fed them as if they were her own children. She was a widow and her only son, Tom Hardie, was a sailor at sea. In those days, before newspapers existed in their present nature, before there were reporters and press-photographers, an event like the appearance of the green children soon ceased to be a matter of more than local interest. It is true that there were many enquiries, and for a long time the green children were pointed out as an object of curiosity to visitors. A doctor from a neighbouring town made an attempt to examine the children in a scientific manner: he wished to take their pulses, sound their lungs, listen to the beat of their hearts, even to do much more scientific things, such as analyse their water and take a specimen of their blood. But Mrs. Hardie was a jealous stepmother, and kept the green children inviolate from such investigations. It was through the action of this disappointed doctor that the legal position was enquired into; but it was found that there was no treasure trove in green children, that the law did not in any way provide for such an eventuality as the appearance of two such extraordinary beings; so possession being nine points of the law, Mrs. Hardie was allowed to keep the children *de jure* as well as *de facto*. The only other trouble was with the village parson, who insisted on baptising the children; but the younger child, or the one who was apparently younger (for there was no distinction in their behaviour or degree of knowledge) died as he was being taken to the church, and this so scared the parson and all who had any desire to interfere, that Mrs. Hardie was left in future severely alone. It is true the dead child could not be given Christian burial, but no one raised any objection when Mrs. Hardie decided to bury it on the triangular patch of ground which was to be found where the road from the moors split in two, one half to go direct to the village, the other half to the mill. It was rumoured that a highwayman had once, in the eighteenth century, been buried on this waste land.

The other green child, whom Mrs. Hardie began to call by the prosaic name Sally, grew up in a normal way —that is to say, she took proper nourishment and increased in size. It was always a matter of speculation to say how old the children were at the moment of their appearance. By their physical development you would have said about four or five years; but in spite of the fact that they could not speak and apparently had no natural thoughts, there was an ageless look in their fully formed but miniature faces which defied all such speculations. And though Sally increased in size of stature, the expression and character of her face did not alter at all; so that now, thirty years later, she had the same ageless innocent features which she had when she first appeared. One could only say that everything was on a slightly larger scale.

There were not wanting those who, at the time of the

first appearance of the green children, saw in the whole matter a portent of witchcraft, and some of the more credulous and suspicious of the villagers would gladly have seen the green children destroyed. But this was a time when enlightenment was spreading very rapidly through the country, and with enlightenment comes toleration. Besides, the Green Child did no one any harm: she lived almost unobserved in Mrs. Hardie's cottage—a cottage that stood some way out of the village, with its back to a wood. It is quite possible that for the greater part of the year the Green Child might have wandered about the woods and the fields totally unobserved, because of her protective colouring.

The road between Kneeshaw's home and the village led past Mrs. Hardie's cottage, and every time he passed that way, Kneeshaw thought of the strange child who lived there. Sometimes he would see her, suddenly stirring out of the immobile green background, like a startled moth. But she was so timid that she never spoke to him and it was only sometimes when he met her walking along the road with Mrs. Hardie coming back from the woods with a bundle of kindling-sticks on her back that he could ever get a nearer view of her. Then he would sometimes stop Mrs. Hardie to ask if she had heard from her son Tom lately and in what foreign parts he might be then. And because before he went to sea Tom had been a sort of elder brother to Kneeshaw, Mrs. Hardie would stop for a minute or two and talk to the queer sullen lad. For several years nothing more happened; but then one year, perhaps ten years after the first appearance of the green children, Mrs. Hardie fell in a faint, and she began to feel that her end was not far off. She knew that she must provide for the future of the Green Child, and the only person to whom her thoughts turned was Kneeshaw. Kneeshaw was now a young man of twenty-two; he was sober and energetic, and the little mill kept by his father was often busy night as well as day, grinding corn for the up-dale farmers. Though a woman was greatly to be desired in that household (for Kneeshaw's mother had died when he was born), Kneeshaw had apparently no interest in women, and in spite of the importunity of his father, showed no inclination to take a wife.

The casual meetings on the road became more frequent, and the conversations about Tom much longer. One day as they passed near the cottage it was raining, so Mrs. Hardie asked Kneeshaw to shelter for a while. He went in with them, and the Green Child made them tea. As he watched her silent movements about the room, her shy and delicate flutterings against the firelight, Kneeshaw knew for the first time the anguish and longing for the presence of a woman in his own home, above all, a longing for this creature who belonged to another world—a world so delicate and subdued. He carried her image back to the bleak mill, to the great bare kitchen with its open fireplace and high smoke-blackened rafters.

Mrs. Hardie soon knew from the bashful look in his eyes and the agitated movements of his body, that Kneeshaw was in love, and she smiled on him and encouraged him. But the Green Child herself made no response. Actually she knew nothing of the nature of love, and felt none of the fleshly promptings which accompany the emotions of love in ordinary mortals. Though she had by now learned how to speak in the English language, her knowledge of it was conditioned by the circumstances under which she lived—by the daily life of an old widow woman, with no interests beyond the rather isolated existence she led in the village. There were no books in the house, and Mrs. Hardie did not even read her Bible, from which the Green Child might have learned so much of the history of the world and the passions of men. To tell the truth, Mrs. Hardie could not read, and when one of Tom's rare letters came from the outer world, she had to ask the postman to step in and read it for her, for which service he was always rewarded with a glass of elderberry wine. About every two years Tom came home for a week, but though after a fashion he was an affectionate son, he was only at ease in the company of men, and spent most of his holiday in the village, drinking with old friends at the inn; or perhaps he would walk up the valley to see Kneeshaw. He was glad to think that his old mother had someone in the house to help her and look after her in case of illness, but the girl, to be sure, was a queer fish, and he could make nothing of her. Once he had told his mates in the foc's'le the strange story of the green children, but they had laughed at him for a credulous fool, so he never mentioned it again; and when he came home, he acted as though he knew nothing of Sally's history. He completely ignored her, and she on her part did not find such behaviour unnatural.

Matters had been brought to a precipitate conclusion by the final illness of Mrs. Hardie. One morning she fainted as she rose from her pillow, and remained for a long time unconscious. She was still unconscious when Sally, wondering why she was so long appearing, went up to her bedroom and found her still and white on the bed. Sally did not know anything about death, or its symptoms, so she sat down to wait for the old woman to awake. Presently her eyelids did flicker a little, and a few minutes later she was fully conscious. But she was very scared at what had happened and sent Sally, not for the doctor, whom she despised, but for Kneeshaw. She remained in bed, and when Kneeshaw came, requested him to come up and sit down by her side. She asked him to take a box from a ledge in the chimney, and to open it. Inside were ninety golden sovereigns, a gold filigree brooch and a locket with a wisp of Tom's hair enclosed in it. The brooch was to be Sally's and the locket was to be sent to Tom, but the money, she said, was to be Kneeshaw's if he would go down on his knees and solemnly swear that he would take Sally and marry her, and be good and kind to her all her life. The clock downstairs was striking the hour of twelve whilst Kneeshaw was on his knees, and when he came downstairs the Green Child was standing against the light of the kitchen window, peeling potatoes, and the light shone through her bare arms and fingers and her delicate neck, and her flesh was like flesh seen in a hand that shelters a candle against the air, or the radiance seen when we look at the sun through the fine web of shut eyelids. Kneeshaw carried the box back to the mill and showed the golden sovereigns to his father, and his father readily agreed to the marriage. With so much money they could buy one of the new roller-machines, and so make flour finer than any the village mill could make.

Mrs. Hardie never rose from her bed again, but died one night in her sleep. The Green Child, when she could not wake her, came to fetch Kneeshaw, and he, knowing what had happened, made her stay behind with his father. Then he went to the village and brought the doctor to Mrs. Hardie's cottage, and it was quite true that she was dead—of heart failure, as the doctor certified in due course. She was buried in a pauper's grave,

D

for no money was found in the house; but later her few
bits of furniture were sold by the auctioneer, and with
the money that they brought, the rent was paid and
there were no more questions about her estate. Nor was
there anyone to question Kneeshaw's action in taking
the Green Child for a wife; for though the parson could
not marry them because the Green Child had never been
baptised, there was no one who would bother to interfere with them; they might live together, isolated in an
indifferent world.

Kneeshaw's father lived perhaps five years after the
coming of the Green Child to his house, but he does not
enter any more into the story. He was a very fat old
man, and spent most of his time sleeping in the arm-
chair in a dark corner of the immense kitchen. The only
other occupant of the house was a kitchen-maid. When
the Green Child came, the maid was sent away, but then
Kneeshaw found that the Green Child was so 'gawm-
less,' as he called it, so inapt in domestic affairs, that the
maid had to be engaged again, to do the cooking and
the cleaning. Among the first peculiarities Kneeshaw
discovered in Sally were an inability to go close to a fire,
and a violent distaste for any form of animal flesh. She
was much more susceptible than a normal person to
extremes of heat and cold, and would shrink as if
scalded from a fire two feet away; she could not bear
her hands in hot water, and she even shrank from the
heat of a human body. Her distaste for meat was con-
stitutional; she turned in disgust from the sight of raw
flesh. Trout from the stream she would eat, but always
as a cold dish. She would drink a little milk, but was avid
only of hazel-nuts, sweet-briar and water-cress, and of
all kinds of mushrooms and toadstools.

When it came to describing their personal relations,

Kneeshaw was naturally very diffident: he spoke in phrases that implied more than they stated. His animal instincts were of the same sullen but strong nature exhibited in all his outward behaviour. He was without experience and therefore without the art necessary to educate his companion in the pleasures and duties of marriage. The Green Child was not merely ignorant of normal sexual cravings—she was entirely devoid of them. She fled from Kneeshaw's embraces as from a hot-breathed faun. She fled out into the night, into the woods, into the branches of the acacia tree which strangely existed in this lonely spot, and there the feathery leaves held her in a safe retreat. She liked the cold water of the mill-race, and without shame or hesitation would throw off her frock and float like a mermaid, almost invisible, in the watery element. She did not seem to have any affection for human beings or animals; she never mentioned Mrs. Hardie from the day of her death; she never paid the slightest attention to the retriever dog, the poultry, or the cattle. Only sometimes she would be seen observing intently little birds, especially those which lived near the ground, such as wrens and linnets; she listened to the earth like a blackbird. She did not sing or whistle, or amuse herself with any sounds. Only the sound of rippling water interested her, and she would play for whole days in the pebbly bed of the stream. She was not capable of much physical exercise, and when she had walked two or three miles, was quite exhausted. If she went out, she always walked in the direction of the moors, away from the village. At first Kneeshaw was alarmed when she did not return by nightfall, and would set out with a lantern to find her—finding her always by the side of the stream. She would follow him obediently back to the mill, but

39

as time went by, Kneeshaw would sometimes fall asleep before he had become aware of Sally's absence, and not once, but many times thereafter, she was out the whole night, sitting by the side of the stream. This was less strange than might appear, since she very rarely slept like a normal human being. It is true that for long hours she would sit in a kind of trance, unaware of what was passing before her, but with eyes open. At night-time, when she lay on her bed in the dark, she might have slept; but Kneeshaw had never observed her in a sound slumber, and if she slept at all, slept so lightly that his very approach was sufficient to wake her.

Two events drew Kneeshaw's attention away from the Green Child. One was the death of his father, together with the expanding trade of the mill—the mill absorbed more and more of his time and energy. The other event was less creditable. One summer day he discovered the kitchenmaid asleep in the barn where the hay was kept. She was lying on her back, her limbs open and abandoned. The sudden lust that swept over Kneeshaw met with no resistance, and from that time onwards Kneeshaw's natural desires were completely satisfied by this subordinate member of the household.

This did not, however, leave Kneeshaw completely indifferent to the Green Child. She continued to attract him in a way and for reasons he would have found difficult to analyse. It was perhaps the mystery of her flesh, the possibility of discovering in her a different mode of love; it was partly the simple charm of her behaviour. Olivero, in all his questionings, could not discover how long a state of veneration had lasted; Kneeshaw, naturally, did not wish to expose himself too much, and though Olivero had profited by his long experience of behaviour in all kinds of men, he was somewhat baffled

by a character at once so elementary and so complex as
Kneeshaw. In Kneeshaw primitive instincts were much
stronger than the conventions of civilised life; but this
does not mean that he was necessarily crude. One has
only to think of the complicated taboos of savage races
to realise that the progress of civilisation has not been
entirely a change from simplicity to complexity, from
roughness to polish, from natural to artificial manners.
The degree of humbug, as some might call it, seems to
have remained fairly constant; it is only the component
details that have changed. A progress from complexity
to simplicity would no doubt require a non-human
world, as Olivero was to discover.

This attitude of respect may have been maintained by
Kneeshaw for as long as ten years. But by that time
daily intercourse would have reduced the man's instinctive fear (for that is what his veneration would
really amount to) to a minimum; and meanwhile his
relations with the kitchenmaid may have become stale
and ungrateful. Certainly, at some period several years
before Olivero's return, Kneeshaw had begun to torment
the Green Child. He began by shutting her up in her
room, in the hope of reducing her movements to some
regularity. If only, he had felt, he could make her sleep
and eat at the normal hours, perhaps she would grow
more human and tractable. At first she escaped again
and again—either through the window, or, when that had
been barred, by the chimney, which was wide enough to
admit her slight and sinuous body. On these occasions
she would disappear for many days at a time, but some
fear kept her from venturing too far from the district,
and her body, wild and exhausted, was always recovered
by Kneeshaw from the moors, where in the side of a hill
she would have made a bed of heather and bracken.

Even when she had been successfully caught, difficulties arose. Kneeshaw turned the attic into a prison. There, though she drank water and milk and a portion of such herbs and salads and cold fish as they brought to her, she visibly wasted. One day they found her in the semi-darkness battering with her delicate fists against the boards which Kneeshaw had nailed across the window. She had fainted in the attempt, and alarmed, Kneeshaw had carried her frail body downstairs, and laid her on the sofa in the room they called the parlour. He was alarmed to see the change that had taken place in her; her flesh had turned from its green translucent colour to a waxen yellow, the colour of ripe golden plums. Her eyes had darkened: her breathing was scarcely perceptible. For a long time she lay there, and in the strong light which flooded in upon her, seemed to revive a little. Kneeshaw left her there to sleep on the sofa that night, and when he came down the next morning, very early, he found her standing in the embrasure of the window, in the first rays of the sun. Her natural tint had returned, and that day she ate again and so gradually regained her strength. She never returned to the dark room upstairs.

When she was strong enough, Kneeshaw took her out into the fields and along the banks of the stream. They spent many long hours in this way, not happy together, because the Green Child had almost ceased to speak and wandered about self-contained, whilst Kneeshaw was suspicious and vigilant. But such excursions were difficult for him, and became increasingly so with the continued expansion of his business. About this time the old mill in the village closed down; Olivero's father's successors were unenterprising and had finally succumbed to the competition of Kneeshaw's mill. Kneeshaw installed a foreman, but the mill had to work such long hours, often through the night, that Kneeshaw himself had to take his share of the day in the mill; and, besides, there was now so much else to do—the markets to visit, the farmers to interview, books and accounts to make up. In none of these operations could the Green Child assist him; her very presence at most times would be embarrassing. There was an increasing number of people about the place—labourers, carters, farmers from up the dale and down the dale. The history of the Green Child was known to all these people; perhaps every man, woman and child within a radius of thirty miles knew of her presence in this world. She was therefore the object of much curiosity and enquiry, all of which Kneeshaw deeply resented. It became known that the miller was touchy on the matter, but still there were always facetious or ignorant people who would not let it rest.

When the routine of life carries a man through the days and months and years, it is surprising how long a state of mental tension may persist. People who are not occupied, whose minds are not, as we say, 'taken off' their troubles, must quickly come to the climax of their emotional experience. But a man like Kneeshaw could let years pass in a state of psychological futility, simply because his mind was so occupied with practical activities, that it automatically excluded personal adjustments. The psychology of the Green Child was a different matter; in a sense, it did not exist. There was no evidence that she possessed any ordinary human affection; at the death of Mrs. Hardie, as already mentioned, she had betrayed no grief—she had not even mourned for the brother she lost. Her reactions in more habitual emotional situations were obvious, but physically odd.

Anger and astonishment she did not show by any vocal or facial expression, but in a trembling of the limbs and a clouding of her translucent flesh; joy was expressed by an increased radiance of flesh, by a bright onyx flame in her eyes, and by a laughter which was a soft crooning sound at the base of her throat. Sorrow, like affection, she did not seem to know, but fear and repugnance produced that blanching or etiolation of the flesh which was the effect of depriving her of the sunlight, but produced it suddenly, like an inverse blush. This leaves the emotion of love still unaccounted for, and that, of course, was the emotion which Kneeshaw had sought vainly to arouse in her. He could not conceive that anything so feminine (and therefore so strongly attractive to his masculinity) could be without what we in the learned world call sexual characteristics, and the blind motive of all the attention he devoted to the Green Child had no other origin. It was a research into the mystery of the Green Child's heart.

But pursued in a dumb instinctive fashion.

Kneeshaw did not convey all these details to Olivero that night, as they sat with the Green Child unconscious in the chair beside them. But as the situation that must have existed for the last five or even ten years became clearer, Olivero grew sick with anxiety. The man who spoke to him, who answered his questions in a sullen unwilling manner, was the boy who thirty years ago had symbolised for Olivero the evil destructive instinct which lurks beneath the civilised conventions of society. In his mood of youthful despair, the sight of this boy deliberately breaking the spring of an intricate toy had precipitated the final crisis of his disillusionment, and with that image burnt into his mind, he had left the scenes of his childhood. Though his subsequent experience had taught him to moderate his despair, even to accept evil as a necessary agent of good, an irritant to stir the slothful soul to action, yet nothing had diminished his sense of the actuality and power of evil. As Kneeshaw spoke, he began to realise, with almost unbearable anguish, that once again the instinctively evil boy had had an intricate machine in his hands, and as he turned to the frail figure in the chair, he feared that once again the spring had been deliberately overwound.

When he had finished questioning Kneeshaw—or rather, when he could no longer bear the pitiful sight of the frail figure lying exhausted in the lamplight—he proposed that they should carry her to her room. Kneeshaw suggested that they should put her on the couch in the parlour, since she liked that room the best, where she would wake in the morning with the sunlight streaming in upon her. So telling Kneeshaw to precede him with the lamp, Olivero went over to the chair and picked up the Green Child in his arms. He was amazed at the lightness of her body, much lighter than the body of a child, lighter than a sheaf of corn. The parlour was on the other side of the vestibule, to the right of the window through which Olivero had made his entrance. It was full of a musty fragrance that came from the unused furniture, the jars of dried rose-petals on the mantelpiece, the bleached sprays of honesty. Inside the shining brass fender were two large and convoluted shells, from whose pink lips a very distant sea murmured continually. Kneeshaw placed the lamp on the circular table in the middle of the room, and Olivero came in with his burden and placed her on the couch, which was already drawn across the window embrasure. He took cushions from the chairs and very gently disposed her head and arms. Olivero looked out into the bright night and wondered whether he should draw the shutters, but, remembering her love of the sunlight, thought that perhaps even the moon's weaker rays might be of some comfort to her, so left them. She was now lying stretched between the lamplight and the moonlight, breathing gently, the fair tresses of her hair catching the light about a waxen face whose peaked misery went straight to Olivero's heart. He stood watching her, something of the fierceness and unrest of his life suddenly quenched in this unearthly coolness.

When he looked up it was to see Kneeshaw's face glaring at him from the space beyond the lamp. He had remained standing there ever since he placed the lamp on the table; his hand still rested loosely on the table-edge. He watched Olivero intently and jealously. The suspicion and resentment that had mounted in his sullen nature all during the questioning to which Olivero had submitted him were now resolved into hatred of the intruder. Olivero's assurance, the mastery with which his mind moved among complexities of character and motive only dimly apprehended by the simpler man, angered Kneeshaw. He foresaw that Olivero would quickly acquire an ascendancy over the Green Child, that he would know how to deal with her, how to speak to her, how to make her human. What he had striven to do through the fruitless years, this man would accomplish in a night.

'Let us go back,' suggested Olivero. 'Bring the lamp.'

He walked out of the room, and Kneeshaw followed obediently enough. They returned to the living-room, and then stood facing each other, Olivero with lowered head, his hands clasped behind his back, quietened by the obvious fatality of the situation; Kneeshaw waiting and watchful.

Presently Olivero jerked himself out of his reverie and addressed Kneeshaw.

'It is now too late to return to the village. If I may, I will stay here until morning.'

'There is no spare bed,' returned the other man.

'It does not matter. I can rest in one of these chairs.'

Kneeshaw moved uneasily. Olivero's persistence had inflamed his temper. He wished to be rid of this man who threatened to disturb the sheltered plan of his life—threatened, even, to take the Green Child from him. 'You must go,' he cried, his clenched fists working up and down like hammers.

Olivero realised that he must keep calm, must appear to yield to the other's persistence. At the same time, he would not leave the Green Child. He had come too far and endured too much to be thwarted of his destiny at this hour of fulfilment.

'Very well,' he said. 'I will go.'

But he did not intend to go. He did not know exactly what he should do. He glanced at the window, but shuddered inwardly. He decided to seek the stream again, beyond the mill. It could not be, of course, that any machinations of Kneeshaw's could have diverted the current, but he would like to have the mental satisfaction of knowing that the stream continued its perverse course beyond the mill. He passed out through the door at the back of the room, Kneeshaw standing sullenly aside. He went through the kitchen and found himself in a paved yard, with dim shadows of trees in the distance before him. But to the left stood the mill, a narrow building three storeys high, its windows dimly lit. The hum of the machinery came softly across the darkness, with the more distant sound of swirling water behind it.

Olivero walked past the end of the mill, past the door through which he saw a twinkle of wheels and a swing of belts, and came to the other end. Here the stream was dammed, and the water sank swiftly and almost silently under the road at his feet. It emerged on the other side of the road, in a sluice down which it ran like a swift bolt of steel, and was shot with force into the pockets of the great mill-wheel. Olivero passed through a small wicket-gate that led on to a platform above the mill-wheel; on his right was a door into the mill. The mill-wheel seemed to move slowly under the great weight of descending water, which broke into angry spray against the dull resistance of the cumbrous wheel. Down below the surplus water from the dam escaped along a steep chute. Beyond the wheel all the waters united again in a tormented whirlpool, from which a roar came up that deadened all other sounds.

Olivero went to the far end of the small platform and looked down into the confused waters. The moon was still sufficient to cast an oily sheen on the water, but Olivero could see no direction in the whirlpool: the falling water had in many years gouged out a deep pool, and one might look into this pool for a whole day without seeing its hundreds of cross-currents repeat a single pattern. It was a continual interweaving of irregular ribbons of water, gushing and spouting in every direction. The final drift of the stream was now lost in the darkness.

Into the darkness Olivero peered, but it was all so hopeless. If for a moment he might stop the mill-wheel, it might be possible to see what happened to the water in the pool. Olivero knew, from his own childhood spent at a mill, that it was the easiest thing in the world to stop a mill-wheel. You had either to move the wooden trough down which the water descended to the wheel, so that its stream fell free of the wheel; or you could close the sluice itself and so cut off the stream of water. After some deliberation, Olivero decided that the latter method would be the better; it would leave the pool less agitated. He therefore returned to the bridge, where the lock controlling the sluice was placed. He was now once more so intent on the solution of his original problem, that he did not realise his action would stop the mill and so betray him.

He screwed down the lock until it would screw no farther, and then rushed back to the platform. The wheel was slowly coming to a standstill, the water dripping from its sodden moss-hung rungs and staves. To get a better view of the pool, Olivero lay flat on his belly, shading his eyes from the rays of the moon. He gazed down into the waters, concentratedly. The waters below still made so much noise, that he was not aware of the cessation of the mill's machinery, and did not even hear the door behind him open. But whilst Olivero was making his researches, Kneeshaw had returned to the mill, and was presently amazed to find his machinery coming to a standstill. The foreman had now left, and therefore no one could have disengaged the mill-wheel. The flow of water must have been diverted, and he therefore made his way to the platform to investigate. When he opened the door, at first he could see nothing, but he noticed that the water from the sluice was not running. He therefore stepped out on to the platform, and in doing so stepped on Olivero's foot. He pitched forward and fell, and since the platform was narrow, and had no hand-railing, he only saved himself from falling headlong over the side of the wheel by clutching at the wooden chute. When he recovered himself and turned, and stood up again, he found himself confronted by Olivero, who had risen in surprise. Olivero was just preparing to shout an explanation above the seething of the water when he saw Kneeshaw's face advance in the light from the open mill door. It was distorted with intense fury and hate, and in a flash Olivero realised that he was going to be attacked. He sprang for the space between Kneeshaw and the open door, but Kneeshaw sprang too, and they closed in a grip on the platform. Kneeshaw had clasped his arms round Olivero's body and was attempting to lift him off his feet and carry him to the edge of the platform. Olivero struggled and succeeded in getting his right arm free and this he pressed palm upwards, with all his force against Kneeshaw's chin, hoping to make him release his grip. But he felt himself being lifted off the ground in spite of all his efforts. Kneeshaw tried to turn with his burden, and Olivero seized the opportunity, when his opponent's balance was all on one leg, of suddenly hurling his weight forward, kicking backwards against the wall of the mill. Kneeshaw staggered and fell across the platform. His head hung over the pit, but he still gripped Olivero like a snake. Olivero spread out his legs to guard against being turned over, and found a buttress for each foot, one against the wall of the mill, the other against the chute. It would be practically impossible for the strongest man to overturn him. With his disengaged hand he was still pressing back the hard foul chin of Kneeshaw, and now he pressed with all his force. He knew that in this way he could break his neck, but he did not wish to go to such an extremity.

'Give in,' he cried, using the phrase he had used as a boy. 'Give in!'

He could not see Kneeshaw's face, which was foreshortened, but he took a relaxing of his grip to mean that he had no wish to struggle any longer. Olivero got up and stood leaning against the open doorway to recover his breath. For a moment or two Kneeshaw did not move, but then he lifted his head up and drew himself into a crouching attitude on the platform. He was breathing heavily—like a doomed bull, Olivero thought as he turned away into the mill. He sat down on a bin near the door, uncertain what to do, but resolved above all things not to leave the Green Child to the mercy of this madman. Presently he saw the dark figure of Kneeshaw cross the open doorway in the direction of the sluice; he had gone, with a kind of animal simplicity, to complete his original intention to set the mill going again. Olivero heard the water swish down the chute and break over the wheel; but since the gear had not been disengaged, the wheel would not move. It had to be released first, and gather momentum before the machinery would engage. Kneeshaw reappeared at the door with this purpose in mind. The lever and gear were directly behind the bin on which Olivero was seated, and at first Kneeshaw hesitated to pass him. But Olivero, understanding his intention, signalled to him to go past.

Kneeshaw pulled the lever and his hand remained resting on it. It was a bar of iron about three feet long, with a square socket at the end which fitted on to the wheel-gear. It lifted off. Outside the mill-wheel gathered momentum. Kneeshaw turned rapidly, the lever lifted above his head. But Olivero had heard the intent interval during which Kneeshaw stood transfixed by the sudden temptation the iron in his hand presented to him, and just as Kneeshaw lifted the lever he turned. Kneeshaw had no time to divert the blow, which fell aimlessly through the air. Olivero sprang back. The lunge of the blow carried Kneeshaw's body staggering forward and for a moment it seemed that his head would butt into the pit of Olivero's stomach. But Olivero had lifted his right foot to ward off the collision and kicking with force, sent Kneeshaw ricocheting through the open door. He saw him tottering backwards on his heels and was about to bang the door in his face when a wild cry rose above the sound of the rushing water and he saw Kneeshaw's body fall backwards into the well beyond the wheel. Olivero dashed out and peered down into the swirling waters. He could see nothing for the spray of the chute, and therefore ran to cut off the flow at the sluice. This done he ran back. The wheel was coming to a standstill again, but as it rose the face of Kneeshaw suddenly emerged out of the obscurity of the well into the moonlight. He was clinging to one of the rungs of the wheel, and rose as the wheel turned. But when he was within three feet of the top of the platform, the wheel finally stopped. He lifted his face to Olivero and cursed him. For now the wheel, being disengaged from the gears and revolving freely on its axis, began slowly to be borne down in the reverse direction by the weight of Kneeshaw's body. Kneeshaw realised that this would happen, and imagined that Olivero knew too, and had stopped the water deliberately. He tried to stop the wheel by wedging his foot against the wall of the platform, but this was all slimy with water weeds and offered no resistance. The wheel suddenly lurched downwards and Kneeshaw fell backwards into the whirlpool. Olivero, who had fallen flat on his stomach in an effort to catch hold of Kneeshaw, saw him fall, and heard his cry, but then the darkness of the well and the tossing water hid everything from his view. He ran back over the bridge, through the stackyard, round to a point where the waters emerged from the wheel-pit. But it was some distance round, for the river at this point ran through a built-up cutting. Olivero waded into mid-stream. The water still swirled round him in tormented coils, but all was dark and invisible in the direction of the mill-wheel. He waded upwards between the black walls, till the water beat against his breast and he felt himself sinking quickly beyond his depth. The roar of water was deafening and nothing could be seen except the dim phosphorescence of the foam. He desisted and made his way back to the low bank. He crouched low, gazing across the surface of the water, to catch sight of any floating object that passed him. But nothing came. He began to shudder violently from the icy cold wet clothes that clung to his skin.

When he could no longer endure the icy agony of the cold, he returned to the house. In the kitchen he found the embers of a fire, before which he stripped and dried and warmed himself. He wrung out his dripping clothes and hung them to dry. In the passage he found an overcoat of Kneeshaw's, and wrapping this round himself, he sank into a chair by the fireside.

He felt sure that Kneeshaw was drowned. It was very unlikely that he could swim, and the pool below the wheel was deep, the currents strong. The mill had stopped; the lights in the lamps would burn low. It must now be two or three o'clock in the morning. At six or earlier the servant girl would come down and find him there. It would be difficult to explain his presence to her; more difficult still to explain Kneeshaw's absence.

But actually he never saw the servant girl. About six o'clock he awoke with a start. It was already daylight, but not a sound was to be heard in the house. He quietly put on his dry clothes and went through to the front vestibule and tapped on the parlour door. There was no sound, so he gently opened the door. The Green Child was up and standing, as Kneeshaw had described her, in the embrasure of the window, as if to catch the first feeble rays of the rising sun.

She looked up without betraying any surprise or emotion. Olivero advanced and took her hand; it was very cold. 'Let us go out into the sun,' he said. She relaxed in her attitude and prepared to follow him. He did not return through the kitchen, but unbarred the disused front door, which led directly to the paddock. The sun was not far risen, but shone warmly above the low meadow mists, the grass heavily laden with dew, the delicate gossamer webs in the hedges. They went across the paddock in the direction of the river. The rabbits scampered away before them, and a few old crows rose croaking from their morning meal.

The green girl walked like a fairy. Her feet were bare and wet with the dew; she looked always up to the sun. A soft cool breeze rippled across her tresses, and agitated the folds of her skirt.

'Kneeshaw has gone,' said Olivero, after some time had passed, and as they approached the river-bank.

She turned an unmoved and perhaps uncomprehending face towards him.

'Kneeshaw has gone,' he repeated. 'He fell into the mill dam, into the water below the wheel. I think he is drowned.'

She said nothing. They were by the side of the stream now, at a point about two hundred yards below the mill. The stream, noticed Olivero, still ran in the direction of the moors.

A grassy path led alongside the stream, which here ran rather deeply between earthy banks. At intervals willow trees grew into the bank; their branches often combed the water.

At the end of the paddock a pole from which was suspended a loose wire grid ran across the stream, to prevent cattle straying up the stream from the field beyond.

In the hedge there was a stile, which they must cross.

Olivero helped the Green Child over the stile. As she turned to cross the top bar, she looked down into the stream, and started.

Olivero followed her startled glance.

In the angle made by the bank and the pole across the stream, in a backwater thick with dried stalks and withered sedge, floated the body of Kneeshaw.

It was face upward, and seemed to look towards them as they stood transfixed by the stile. His black hair, wet and matted, fell over his pale forehead, but did not hide the wide and staring eyes.

Olivero, in spite of all his experience of death and terror, was deeply horrified. He had already concluded that Kneeshaw was drowned, but the sudden sight of his dead body actualised, in one acute instant, all the mental distress of the last twelve hours.

But the Green Child was already moving on. She had, before he had realised it, descended from the stile and taken a few steps in apparent unconcern. She did not look back, but went slowly on.

With one last look at the corpse swinging in the current of the stream, Olivero leapt over the stile and followed the Green Child. They walked several miles, past the outlying farms, and at last left the fields and followed the stream, now diminished, across the moorland.

But how can the stream grow narrow and yet flow onwards? Olivero asked himself. He explained his perplexity to the Green Child, but she merely walked on. Olivero was now exhausted with lack of sleep and hunger, but the Green Child had revived as the sun rose. They drank water from the stream, and at a place on the moor where the stream forked, and three pine trees cast some shade, they rested for two hours, and during that time Olivero told the Green Child the story of his life.

Then in the afternoon they followed the stream into the heart of the moor. About four o'clock they came into a small valley, near the highest point of the moorland. It had an entrance, but no exit. At the farther end it curved round, and there in the basin at the foot of this slope, the stream had its beginning, or its end.

Olivero's heart beat with excitement as he approached the end of his long research. It seemed so long, a whole lifetime, since he had left the village the evening before on this errand of investigation. Here he was at the solution of his perplexity. The stream came to an end here, not in the all-gathering sea, but far inland, in the embrace of the hills.

Olivero took off his shoes and socks, and rolling up his trousers, waded out into mid-stream. The bed of the stream was warm and sandy; his feet sank into the warm sand. The Green Child followed him, and side by side they walked towards the basin. The stream expanded into a bog, thick with rushes and myrtle. Soon they saw before them a round pool. The stream flowed into this pool, and seemingly round it, in a complete circle. But the middle of the pool was very still, no vortex. There were even lilies and kingcups floating on the surface. It must be shallow, thought Olivero, but where, then, does the water go? They advanced slowly. The water moved softly against their limbs. It was slightly warm, like the sandy bed. They were now near the point at which the current, having described its circle, met itself. A bed of clear silvery sand stretched before them. Olivero bent down and looked closely. The sand, though it seemed solid, was vibrating, each grain dancing like a tiny silver ball on a stretched drum. The water, thought Olivero, must sink here.

And as he thought this, he saw the green naiad figure of Sally step forward. She walked swiftly through the water on to the silvery sand. She was sinking, and as she sank she turned towards Olivero. Her face was transfigured, radiant as an angel's. She stretched out an arm towards Olivero. With a cry of happiness, as if a secret joy had suddenly been revealed to him, he raced forward and hand in hand they sank below the surface of the pool.

2

THE story that Olivero related to the Green Child when they rested under the pine trees died on the moorland air. The narrative that follows is based on the papers which were discovered afterwards in the baggage he had left at the inn, reinforced by the archives of the Hispanic Association of South America. Naturally it lacks the simplicity of style which Olivero must have used on that unique occasion; for he would realise, as he spoke to the Green Child, that she came from a world of which he had no knowledge. She had never been able to describe that world to anyone, because there were no earthly words to exchange for her memories. If he had asked her if trees like those above them grew in that world, or if any trees at all grew there, she would only have shaken her head and said: 'Everything was different.'

For thirty years Olivero, too, had lived in a world where everything differed strangely from the peaceful scene before them. Trees grew in that country, of course, as in England, but their green leaves were often covered with white dust, and hung in the glaring sun like leaves of clay. Olivero had words like these to describe his world, too many words, words the Green Child had never heard and could not understand. But he had to use those words, because words and things grow together in the mind, grow like a skin over the tender images of things until words and things cannot be separated. The words the Green Child did not understand fell like music on her ears, and the music had a meaning for her, so that none of Olivero's words was altogether lost on the moorland air.

When I left our village thirty years ago, he began, I

made my way first to London, because London was the centre of the world, and I thought that among all its wonders, in the variety of its ways, I should find my appointed place. I had faith in certain of my talents. I was ambitious—that is to say, I was anxious to win command over men by the exercise of those talents—talents for writing, for expressing ideas, for using words. Words can be bright and glittering, can attract men's eyes and fascinate their minds—even when they mean little or nothing. But I did not realise how difficult it would be to make one's voice heard, to lift one's self above the crowd, to gain any little eminence from which the words might attract attention. I wandered from one newspaper office to another, but nowhere was it possible to gain entrance, to make a beginning. I had nothing to offer them—a young country schoolmaster, who had never published a line, who had no experience of newspaper work.

The twenty pounds I had brought with me were soon exhausted. At first I allowed myself a pound a week to live on, but when ten weeks had passed, with no work in sight, I then allowed myself only ten shillings a week. And when another ten weeks had passed, and still no work found, then I allowed myself five shillings a week, sleeping in beds that cost sixpence a night and spending the rest on bread. I was in this unhappy condition when one day I saw a notice in a tailor's shop window, which read: 'SMART YOUTH WANTED. APPLY WITHIN.' It was a raw November day. I was cold and hungry: I entered the shop. Facing me was a counter, and behind it a room stacked with rolls of cloth down one side; on the other side was a staircase leading to an upper floor, and underneath the staircase an office separated from the room by a wood and glass partition. The door of this office opened with a click, and a man advanced towards me—Mr. Klein, the owner of the shop. He was a small man with a big head sunk low in his shoulders; his skin was grey and loose on his rounded jaws; the lids of his eyes were lashless. There was something like a snake in his general appearance—a squat reptile, a tortoise. I drew myself up as he approached me. I was tall in comparison, and was then very thin and emaciated; my hair had grown long and fell in a shock over my forehead and ears.

I explained that I was an applicant for the post advertised in his window. He looked at me sharply and asked my age. I said nineteen, because a man already twenty is perhaps no longer to be called a youth. 'Oh, too old!' Mr. Klein exclaimed, waving his fat wrinkled hands impatiently.

'But no!' I cried, and there must have been something compelling enough in my desperate voice to make Mr. Klein check the backward turn which he had already given to his body, and raise his eyebrows in surprise.

'I am young, I am starving, I can work hard,' I began to explain.

'Are you clever with figures?' he asked, in a voice which I then recognised as foreign.

'Yes. I was at a good school. I have studied mathematics,' I explained, not wishing to put my claims too high.

'Mathematics, eh? Mathematics!' cried Mr. Klein, and that was, I think, the first time I had exercised the magic power of words, of one word! 'So you have studied mathematics. Well, perhaps we can do business.' And then he asked several other questions, and finally agreed to give me a trial. I was to return at eight o'clock the next morning.

That night I gave myself a good meal, and next morning, in a clean collar which I had bought, I reported myself to Mr. Klein. I had pretended to know how to keep books, but my only knowledge was a dim remembrance from my school days. But I trusted to my general intelligence to pull me through, and in the end I was justified. Mr. Klein was a Jew from Poland, who had fled to England several years before this time. At first he had worked as a tailor's cutter, but being of a capable and independent nature, had quickly saved enough money to begin on his own account. When I walked into his shop, he had been in business for only six months, and during that time had attempted to keep his own books. But the English money system gave him great trouble, and many hours were spent in fruitless endeavour to make his accounts balance. So finally he decided to employ a clerk, and had put a notice in his window only an hour or two before I had seen it. I was the first applicant for the post, and was, after my first day's trial, engaged at a salary of one pound a week.

The first day I spent checking Mr. Klein's books, and he was so impressed with the rapidity and sureness with which my eye added up the columns of pounds, shillings and pence, that he made no further enquiry into my capabilities. For myself I found that my school knowledge sufficed for the simple business of balancing the credit and debit sides of Mr. Klein's cash-book and ledger, and with this he was perfectly satisfied. When he further asked for an analysis of his costs, I was able to give him this without difficulty. In a week or two I had established a relationship of complete confidence and was even given control of the cash-box.

I shall not trouble you with any further details of this part of my life. I grew to like Mr. Klein, to understand his simple commercial mind, to sympathise with the background of racial persecution which explained his presence in London and was the motive for his desire to justify himself in the world. I discovered, for example, his intense family loyalty. He had left behind in Poland an old mother and two sisters. It was his ambition to make a home for them in England; but it must be a good home, a place of comfort which would give them a standing in the world, where the family could be re-established with himself as the patriarchal head. But I did not stay with him long enough to see his ambition realised. Actually I had loathed the dingy shop, the smell of cloth, the pervading greasy odour of the district, the dull unimaginative work I was compelled to do, the general poverty of my circumstances. Poverty is de-grading for any human being; but for one born with those instincts and senses which cry out for beauty and sensitive pleasures, for music and poetry and romance, it is a slow torture, a torture of the mind rather than of the body, and so all the more acute. There were mo-ments, passing before a bookshop or a theatre, when the gall seemed to rise in floods of bitterness within me. I envied the people who could afford to indulge their senses to satiation—people who could take these things for granted, as part of their routine and heritage, and without the real need that consumed me. I did not cry so much against the society in which this unjust distri-bution of goods was normal, but rather saw the problem as an individual one, and longed myself to possess the power to command such things. Perhaps in this I was no better than my employer, Mr. Klein; but I was less practical. Mr. Klein knew that possession is only given in exchange for the tokens of wealth, which are earned by industry; and therefore set himself single-mindedly to accumulate these tokens. I wished to possess myself of power directly, by virtue of my personality and intelligence, and therefore I was restless and unhappy. I wished to escape.

I had entered into a bond to serve Mr. Klein for three years, and in virtue of this bond he had increased my salary, first to thirty shillings a week, and finally to two pounds. During the last two years of my service with him I managed to save—altogether I saved forty pounds, and with this sum I determined, at the end of my bondage, to venture out into the world.

At first my thoughts turned to America, where so many young men in my situation had ventured with success. But my longings, though romantic, had definite limitations; they were not of the kind that finds a satisfaction in struggling with natural forces. I was not a pioneer by instinct, but sought rather to dwell in those countries and cities where the longest human experience had left the richest deposit of beauty and wisdom. Greece, Italy, Spain were the scenes of my most frequent fancies, and if my thoughts ranged farther, it was to the remote and mystical East, to India and China. Actually it was Mr. Klein himself who set me off on my wanderings. I think he realised the deep-seatedness of my unrest, and when I confided to him that I intended to seek my fortune abroad, he was not merely sympathetic, but entrusted me with a mission which took me to the heart of Europe. Though the letters he received from his sisters gave him no cause for alarm, he wished to be assured of the well-being of his mother, who could not herself write. He wished also to transmit to her a sum of money, about a hundred English pounds, but would not trust the post with such a sum. His mother lived in a small town to the south of Warsaw, and thither Mr. Klein proposed to send me, paying the expenses of my outward journey and giving me ten pounds in addition, to carry me farther if I wished. I accepted his offer without hesitation; during my three years in London I had made no friends I particularly cared for, and there was nothing, nothing at all, to keep me in England. It was already October when we began to discuss this plan, and at first Mr. Klein suggested that I should wait for the next spring, when travelling would be pleasanter. But so eager was I to be away on such an adventure, that I would not hear of such a delay, and one day in November, almost exactly three years after I had first entered Mr. Klein's shop, I left London for Warsaw.

I did not delay on the outward journey. The money, in gold coins, was strapped round my middle in a belt which Mr. Klein himself had made. The trains in those days were few, slow and uncomfortable, and I was travelling in the cheapest possible manner. Nevertheless, no words could convey the interest and excitement with which I followed every stage of the journey—the coast of England receding as we set out to sea, the sense of being at sea, the first impact of foreign voices and foreign faces at Hamburg, where I left the ship, the strange habits of my companions in the coach which I took to Lubeck, the bustle and renewal of interest at every stage. I sat still and silent in a corner of the coach. I was conscious of the belt under my shirt. I slept fitfully. At Lubeck I took a small coasting vessel to Danzig, from whence I proceeded by boat up the River Vistula, until the ice made navigation impossible. The last part of my journey was accomplished in a sleigh, drawn by small shaggy ponies. When we reached Warsaw it was intensely cold; snow had fallen and under its white covering the houses and streets looked like pictures in a book of fairy-tales. But the reality was grimmer. In the large square where I went to find the coach for N——, the town where Mr. Klein's mother lived, a large crowd was gathered. I joined one of their ranks and waited. Presently a stir and a murmur swept across the waiting people, and from one side of the square a group of mounted soldiers approached, holding long spears in their right hands, with rifles slung across their backs. They were followed by a cart drawn by four horses, escorted on each side by another mounted soldier; two other soldiers followed on foot, with rifles only. The cart was boarded across to make a platform, and on this platform, seated on a bench, was a poor dejected wretch of a man. He was clad in a cap and greatcoat, and round his neck was hung a board, inscribed with two lines of black lettering. I could not read this notice, and could not make enquiries from those about me; but there was no need. It was only too evident that the man was a condemned criminal on his way to the gallows. Some of the crowd near me shouted out angry jeering words, but the prisoner paid no attention. A few flakes fell out of a cold grey sky; the procession passed, oddly silent on the fallen snow.

I could not speak the Polish language, but Mr. Klein had given me a letter which I could show to anyone who looked kindly and sympathetic, explaining that I was an Englishman who wished to proceed to the town of N——, and requesting the kind stranger to assist me. With this letter, and a few words which I had learnt, I found the coach without difficulty and eventually reached N——. The house of the Kleins was in an obscure side street, but this, too, I found without great difficulty, and for the situation I now had to face the letters I carried with me were sufficiently explanatory. I was welcomed at the door by one of Klein's sisters, and led through into a dark kitchen where a very old wrinkled woman was seated in the corner of an immense pottery stove. She was deaf, and muttered unintelligibly; but I was presently shown to a bedroom, which I gathered would be put at my disposal for as long as I cared to stay. When I had washed myself, I returned to the kitchen and laid the belt of money on the table, not a little relieved to have reached my destination and fulfilled my mission. The old woman turned her chair to the table, and without a moment's hesitation began to unpick the belt with a knife. The gold coins were revealed one by one, and piled up in neat order. Only when the last coin had been recovered did the old woman again become aware of my presence, and then, to my alarm, she rose from her chair and stumbled across to where I was seated, pressed her hands on my head and kissed my brow in gratitude. She then took a silk cloth, gathered the money into it, and disappeared upstairs. Meanwhile the sister (only one ever appeared, and I concluded that the other was married and had left the house) had prepared a meal. Whilst we ate, the two women talked to each other in happy excited voices, almost ignoring my presence except when they turned with smiles to press more food on me. I stayed three days with them, resting all the time, deliberating much, not yet determined what my next step should be.

The only foreign language I knew at that time was French, but I had no particular desire to go to France. I decided to make my way back to Hamburg and there consider what next to do. I said good-bye to the Klein family, returned to Warsaw, and from there retraced my path without any untoward incident. On the way I thought of every means of earning a living, but I could think of no other way than the one my abilities, coupled with my intention to stay abroad, fitted me—namely, the teaching of my own language to foreigners. At Hamburg, however, an unexpected chance presented itself. I decided to seek the advice of the English consul, on how best to work my way to some cosmopolitan city like Paris. I found a sympathetic man, who after some conversation took interest in my plans, and invited me to sup with him. Eventually, through his kind intervention, I was taken on a vessel trading with Bordeaux and Morocco. It was agreed that I should deposit two hundred and fifty marks, half of all that remained to me, with the captain of the vessel, to be forfeited should I not make the return passage. I was to assist the captain, who was English, as purser and steward.

In spite of my lack of experience, I managed to discharge these duties to the satisfaction of the captain. Besides the first mate, he was the only Englishman on board, the crew consisting of a miscellaneous collection of Poles, Lascars, and Germans. At first I was so pleased with my post, that in spite of the discomfort of such a life, I thought I might endure it for a year or two, whilst I improved my command of the two or three principal languages of Europe. I still thought so when we reached Bordeaux, in spite of the rough seas we encountered in the Bay of Biscay. But when, three or four days later, we reached the port of Cadiz, my resolution suddenly changed. The foul weather we had experienced in the Atlantic Ocean was left behind when we turned Cape St. Vincent; when we entered Cadiz harbour, the air was warm and sweet, the city glittering beyond the blue water, its snow-white turrets rising majestically into the clear sky. I was enchanted by the sight, and when I went on shore, still further delighted by all I saw—the marble streets, the massive ramparts, the wide promenades. At that time the memory of bitter wars was still alive, and the inhabitants of Cadiz in particular had no reason to welcome an Englishman. But I had conceived a romantic affection for our ancient enemies and was therefore overcome with joy to find no resentment among them, but everywhere a carefree gaiety and a manner of life which struck me as ideal. Suddenly I had no desire to travel further. Here I would disembark with my small capital, and seek my fortune.

The captain was furious at my desertion, and naturally I forfeited my bond money. But when I left the ship with my few belongings, he bade me farewell with a good grace, and even gave me a letter of introduction to some merchants in Seville, with whom I might find employment.

Actually, however, I was not destined to leave Cadiz for many months. Ignorant as I was, both of the language of the country and the state of its affairs, I strayed into a trap which perhaps in any case I should not have avoided. On leaving the ship, I had gone to a lodging-house frequented by sailors. I had spent the evening wandering about the town, accustoming myself to its atmosphere, enjoying the strange sights and sounds. Towards midnight I returned to my lodging, and on entering was immediately accosted by three men in uniform. One of them, who appeared to be of some subordinate rank, poured out a torrent of harsh words, not one of which had any meaning for me. But by his gestures I gathered that I was under arrest, and must accompany them.

It was useless to resist. The keeper of the lodging-house, a fat and disagreeable old sailor, looked at me with displeasure. My kitbag, which I had left in an upper room, was in the possession of one of the soldiers.

Bewildered, I turned towards the door, and was then marched through the deserted streets, until we finally arrived at a dark and forbidding building. It was some kind of citadel or barracks, and here I was thrust into a bare room, obviously a prison cell. There was no bed or chair; the floor was of stone. Most of the night I spent pacing up and down, in an endeavour to keep warm. Occasionally I crouched in a corner and dozed until the cold and the cramp forced me to my feet again.

There I stayed, unvisited, until about the midday following. Then I was fetched from my cell, and brought before an officer. He looked at me indifferently and spoke to me in Spanish. Perhaps he asked me whether I could speak Spanish; at any rate, I replied in French that I could not understand that language, and begged him to explain in French the reason of my arrest.

He turned to another officer seated by his side and made some humorous remark in Spanish. Then 'Vous êtes français?' he asked, in an accent I hardly recognised as French. I protested that I was English. 'Et Jacobin,' he added. He then held up a book which I recognised as my property. It was a book by a French writer, Voltaire, a book of great wit and wisdom, which I valued almost above all other books, and constantly read.

In a flash the situation was clearly revealed to me. For many years, Cadiz had been the revolutionary centre of Spain. Here, in 1812, the Cortes met and proclaimed the first Liberal constitution; here, in 1820, to renew that constitution, the citizens revolted, and the revolution had spread throughout Spain. That revolution had later been suppressed by a French army under the duc d'Angoulême, and ever since a state of anarchy and military oppression had existed. So much I knew, but in my innocence I had not realised the state of vigilance and espionage which still persisted, nor the incriminating character of the few books I carried with me.

Though never actively concerned with political affairs, my sympathies were decidedly Liberal. Voltaire, Rousseau and Diderot were authors who appealed to me both by the enlightened nature of their philosophy and the literary graces of their style. I had read other writings of a revolutionary flavour, such as Volney and Montesquieu. When, therefore, this question 'Etes-vous Jacobin?' was suddenly hurled at me, I could not instinctively repudiate the name. I began to explain that I had no connection with the Jacobins, that I had no political beliefs of any kind. But the more voluble I grew, the less convinced the officer became, and he soon cut me short with the further question: 'Ce livre est à vous?'

I could not deny it. Nor could I protest against the flimsy nature of the evidence. I knew that everywhere, particularly among the clergy and the reactionary forces, Voltaire was regarded as the arch-fiend who had first propagated Jacobin doctrines. I stood perplexed and angry. 'Basta!' the officer cried, and gave further orders in his language. I was hurried out of the room and returned to my cell. From there, later on in the day, I was moved to a common prison, where I found myself in the company of about a hundred others, some ordinary rogues, some political prisoners. We were herded together in indescribable filth and squalor; soldiers were scarce and in such circumstances a few armed men could guard a hundred prisoners with ease.

There I remained for the best part of two years. I made many efforts to make myself understood, and to get the injustice of my lot redressed. But until I had learned sufficient of their language to communicate with my gaolers, it was impossible to present my case; and when, after several months' assiduous exercise with my fellow prisoners, I could at last express myself clearly and forcibly, my guilt was regarded as confirmed by time and my acquiescence.

Those dreadful months were to determine my future life. Not only did I become an adept of the Spanish language, but I met, among my fellow prisoners, a number of so-called Jacobins, some of whom had in the past been followers of the famous revolutionary general, Rafael del Riego. As I have already confessed, I began with a certain general sympathy for their point of view; when ambition and poverty are joined in an individual, such a tendency is almost inevitable. But now I came into contact with political realities. I learned of the struggle that had taken place to establish justice in Spain—of Riego's abortive revolt and of Ferdinand's hateful reign. We talked often of the liberated colonies in America, of their democratic constitutions and the possibilities of establishing there a new world free from the oppression and injustice of the old world. The men I talked with were not by any means disinterested idealists; some, indeed, were no better than military adventurers, and though they had acquired, for the purpose they had in view, a certain familiarity with Jacobin doctrines, I had no reason to believe that their rule, should they ever come to power, would be any less tyrannous than that of the existing monarchy. But there were among my acquaintances two or three men of a different cast, men who had been youths at the time of the French Revolution, and who had then become imbued with enthusiasm for the cause of liberty, equality and fraternity. These men gave force and direction to my vague sympathies; in short, they converted me to their cause.

The death of Ferdinand, and the proclamation of the new Queen, was made the occasion of a partial amnesty, from which I benefited. Whilst still in prison I had determined, when once released, to make my way to the free colonies, to seek my fortune in whatever way presented itself. I still had in my possession twenty English guineas, sewn, after my former employer's example, into the lining of my waistcoat. With these I hoped to procure a passage to Buenos Ayres or Rio de Janeiro, failing any method of working my way. On my release, I at once carried out this intention.

The story of my voyage would take too long to tell in full. At Cadiz I enlisted on one of those ships, which under cover of the Spanish flag, intercepted the English trading vessels on their way from the revolted Colonies. In all but name we were pirates, our crew partially recruited from the prison I had just left. At sea, after we had successfully accosted two homeward bound vessels, and deprived them of the best of their cargoes, we were surprised by an outward bound vessel, which gave us chase, and being unburdened and of larger sail, quickly overtook us. We surrendered after the exchange of a futile shot or two, and I should have shared the fate of the rest of the crew, and been put into chains, had I not revealed my nationality and explained my unhappy fate. As it was, I was accepted in good faith by the English captain, and made the go-between and interpreter in all his dealings with the captive vessel. Another English vessel having been sighted, a convoy was formed and the captives conducted to Buenos Ayres, and there handed over to the authorities. I carried out the necessary negotiations for the English captain, and then asked him for my release. He replied by offering me a place with his crew, but I was determined to seek my fortune in the Colonies; and when I had explained my intention to him, I was dismissed with a friendly handshake.

It was late in the day when I left the English ship. I decided to find a lodging near the shore. Avoiding the main thoroughfare as likely to be above my fortune and appearance, I took a parallel but less frequented street, leading from the river bank in the direction of what I judged to be the centre of the town. After Cadiz, I was depressed by the flat and monotonous appearance of the place, and suddenly felt forlorn and helpless. The streets were deserted, and I had to walk for a long time past sheds and quays before reaching the inhabited quarters. Most of the houses were of the familiar Spanish type —presenting blank walls and iron grilles to the street front, occasionally offering, through an open doorway, a glimpse of the bright and flowery patio within. I saw nothing in the nature of a lodging-house, so decided to enter a coffee-house, and whilst having some food and drink, make enquiries from the owner.

No sooner had I made this decision, than I came by a house which differed from the usual type; instead of a patio, the open door led directly to a room, which was lit from a lamp suspended from the ceiling. It was a bare room, but seated round a rough table were several men, drinking wine. In later days, when I thought back on this scene, it occurred to me that several things, but principally the solemn and intent mien of the whole company, should have deterred me; but at the time, tired and hungry, and very uncertain of my surroundings, I took the place for a modest wine-house, such as I had seen in Cadiz and in other parts of Europe. I therefore entered. If you are to understand what followed, you should have some notion of my appearance at that time. My long incarceration had left me with a lean frame, hollow cheeks, and eyes that seemed unnaturally large and dark. On leaving the prison I had acquired a Spanish hat, wide of brim and high in the crown. I wore a dark brown shirt and a red neckerchief, and instead of a coat, carried across my shoulder my sailor's blanket; the few possessions I was left with were tied in a bundle which I carried in my hand. Until I reached the threshold of the room I was unperceived.

I stood there, looking for someone I might address. But no sooner was I noticed than there was a general movement, the men at the table rising to their feet. They greeted me with expressions of welcome, and made a place for me at the head of the table. I was still under the impression that I had entered a public room, and was not a little astonished at the general courtesy and respect shown to me. A glass was placed before me and filled with wine.

I was conscious of a certain expectancy among my companions, but sipped my wine with as much unconcern as I could muster. For a period that seemed an eternity no one spoke. Then a voice from across the table addressed me : 'The Señor has had a good voyage?'

I lifted my gaze slowly, determined to be cautious.

'Yes,' I replied, 'by the grace of God I arrived safely.'

'You came by the English ship that anchored in the estuary this morning?'

'By the same.'

'We expected you yesterday, direct from Cadiz.'

'From Cadiz I came, but the ways of the sea are not direct.'

I answered blindly, at first with the desire to be complaisant. But I had not taken these three steps before I perceived that I had entered on a strange path, which led I knew not whither. Never had I been more conscious of my destiny, that obscure force which drives us to impersonal action, to the surrender of the self to the event.

'It is well,' added the same speaker. And then, as if to echo my thoughts: 'The man of destiny cannot be defeated, not even by the elements.'

We drank in silence again for some time. Then the same man spoke again:

'We have arranged that you shall rest in this house for two days. By the end of that time the guides from Roncador will be here. If you proceed by river the journey will take you many weeks; we therefore advise you to travel on horseback, and then in about twenty days you will reach your destination. You will wait in the hills for the revolutionary forces under General Santos. The rest is unknown.'

By then I was in possession of the facts essential to an understanding of the maze into which the obscure workings of destiny had directed me. The general situation in South America was well known to me from my conversations with my fellow-prisoners in Cadiz. The corruption of the mother country had for many years been reflected, even exaggerated, in her colonial dependencies, ruled for the most part by tyrannous viceroys and captains-general. As a result, a spirit of unrest had grown up among the settlers and natives, against which Spain, distracted by foreign invasion and domestic strife, was powerless to assert herself. Buonaparte's invasion of the Peninsula had been the final act in the fall of an Empire, warning the outer provinces that the time had come for them to assert their independence, and bring into being a new world. Though the doctrines of the French Revolution had penetrated into the American Colonies, in most cases the decisive action was taken by the native militia, and in effect the new republics were ruled by military juntas, to which the Spanish troops hastened to ally themselves. Though the revolutions were in nearly all cases bloodless, there was no continuous peace. The juntas assembled by the various dictators proved ignorant and intractable, and there was not a single colony that was not involved in a period of hopeless discord. But in every colony a few idealists existed, men imbued with the true republican principles, desirous to govern their countries for the benefit of the inhabitants. For the most part small traders, creoles and peasants, they lacked the necessary qualities for political leadership, and were everywhere dependent on somewhat unscrupulous adventurers, generally lawyers who envied the power of the military dictators, and who therefore professed revolutionary principles in the hope of commanding sufficient force to displace them.

The group of men I met in Buenos Ayres was, as I was to learn later, of a somewhat different character. Formed on the model of the Jacobin Club, it had as its object the conversion of the whole of South America to the principles of the Revolution, and the eventual federation of all the former colonies into one Republic. For that purpose it was in communication with the revolutionaries in Spain, from whom it expected to receive accredited agents ready to act as political leaders in the endeavour. By what particular chain of coincidence my own arrival answered to their immediate expectations, I was never to learn. I accepted my fate, and they on their part had no cause to question my good faith.

The spokesman of the group, whom the others addressed as Don Gregorio, asked me many questions relating to the affairs in Spain, more especially those of

Cadiz, from which city he had emigrated on the failure of del Riego's rebellion, and all these questions I was able to answer fully. I discovered, for example, that among my late fellow-prisoners were several who had been Don Gregorio's associates in the past, and of these friends we talked for some time. Then, perceiving that I was weary, Don Gregorio suggested that I should retire to the room that was prepared for me, which I did presently, glad to be alone to consider my position and my future action.

I fell asleep, too exhausted to come to any decision that night, my mind full of doubt and perplexity. I slept long, but often waking in fright and anxiety. My dreams were full of terror, but towards dawn I fell into a deeper slumber, and when I awoke, late in the morning, all this terror was forgotten; my mind was clear and a decision soon made. To retire from the part I was playing seemed to me not only a base desertion of the Providence that had guided me to this spot, but, in sober truth, a dangerous course. If I revealed myself, I should have to confess to the deception I had practised the previous night, with unknown consequences. If I attempted to escape, I should have to reckon with the vengeance of men who had dedicated themselves to desperate measures, and who were not likely to tolerate the existence of a traitor at large. In addition, my actual chances of escape were remote, considering the fact that I was a stranger in the city, with no definite plans and no knowledge of where best to hide or in what way to extricate myself.

I therefore decided to risk the possibility of discovery, and to continue to play the part for which destiny had cast me. I rose, and, when I had washed and dressed, made my way downstairs. In the room where the meeting had been held the previous night I found only an old woman, who helped me to a bowl of coffee and a loaf of bread. I decided not to question her, but to await events. About midday a young Spaniard appeared, whom I recognised as one of the revolutionaries, followed by a native gaucho. The latter was introduced to me as the guide who was to accompany me to Roncador, and with whom I might discuss the plans for the journey, the purchase of necessary equipment and food, and any other details.

This man was an old post-rider, perfectly familiar with the method of travelling in that country, dependable, but not above arranging matters to his personal advantage. I foresaw that I might have to take him into my confidence, and therefore entrusted him with a liberal amount of gold with which to purchase a saddle, pistols and other necessaries, informing him that if he made a good purchase he might have the surplus as a reward. I was still discussing the journey with him when Don Gregorio appeared, and, after adding his advice on some particulars, invited me to dine with him. We went some distance through the streets till we came to a pretty house with a patio or quadrangle, and there we joined Don Gregorio's family (his wife and two small children) at a copious and well-cooked meal, the best food, in fact, that I had tasted for more than two years. During the meal neither my mission nor any other serious affairs were discussed; but afterwards, when the rest of the family had retired to their siesta, Don Gregorio showed me his library, a cool room furnished with a table and a couch, a terrestrial globe and a collection of two or three hundred books, mostly of a political or legal character. We exchanged opinions about some of the volumes he picked from the shelves, and then I was left to take my siesta on the library couch.

It was four or five o'clock before I was again disturbed. Don Gregorio came and told me that I should have to leave Buenos Ayres at dawn the next day, and should now make any further preparations I felt necessary before retiring to my room for all the rest I could obtain. He offered to accompany me to the best stores, and to lend me money should I require any. But there was little that I could think of as appropriate to my adventure. I purchased a pocket compass, some pencils and paper, and various articles of clothing. Don Gregorio accompanied me back to my original lodging, and there said good-bye to me. He gave me messages of fraternal good-will for General Santos, and instructed me in a simple code by means of which I might transmit messages to himself or to any members of the Society in Buenos Ayres.

At four o'clock the next morning the gaucho came to wake me. He had a post horse at the door, with my saddle and equipment already in place. I filled the saddle-bags with my few possessions and mounted with some trepidation. Although from boyhood used to riding horseback, it was three or four years since I had been in the saddle, and never had I ridden the long distances before us. Dawn was just breaking as we clattered through the deserted streets of Buenos Ayres. From my guide I learned that we might expect to cover from sixty to eighty miles a day, but I confided to him that I could not contemplate so much the first day or two. When we reached the first post-house, about twenty miles from the city, I still felt tolerably fresh, and agreed to press on to the next stage. Altogether we rode forty-three miles that day, and put up at the post-house, a miserable thatched hut, with no provision for the traveller beyond a hammock of dried hide, some roasted or boiled beef, and the insipid tea of that country. At each post-house we found a relay of horses, taken from the large herds which are everywhere reared on the pampas. The horses were fresh and almost wild, and covered the ground at a pace far swifter than the horses of this country.

The memory of that journey is still vivid in my mind. It was a new country for me, and I observed everything with interest and excitement. The wide grassy pampas are devoid of natural features, but their level immensity was itself most impressive, even awesome. The grasses and plants that grew by the side of our road were of gigantic size—the thistles in particular rearing their crowns and jagged branches like fantastic trees above our heads. Great herds of cattle moved like migrations over the plain; deer and ostriches bounded from our path, and smaller animals, the bearded biscachas and the mailed armadillo, met our onset with sudden surprise; whilst every few hundred yards a covey of partridges would rise whirring from under our feet.

The people I met on my journey are less distinct, eclipsed in my memory by the more remarkable events of later years. But everywhere I found hospitable men—post-house keepers, farmers, sometimes a priest. My passage was unimpeded—everyone assumed I was a trader, or perhaps a prospector—and for my part I adopted a pleasant but reserved attitude. At two of the larger towns we rested for a day, but at the end of twenty days I reckoned we had come about 1,200 miles, and were within a day's ride of our destination. We were at the foot of a mountain range that stretched as far as the eye could see on either side. The village we had reached, inhabited entirely by Indians, was at the end of the road. To the east the great river, that at a distance of never more than fifty miles had been our constant companion, descended through the mountains in a series of rapids and immense waterfalls, the booming sound of which could be heard in our village. The pass into Roncador was merely a rocky and precipitous track, crossing the ridge about fifty miles to the west of the falls.

On our journey I had had much opportunity to commune with myself, for the gaucho, though agreeable enough as a travelling companion, resourceful and faithful, had no great powers of conversation. He knew that I was bound on a political mission, but I doubt whether this meant anything to him. He had a fixed loathing of the Old Spaniards, as the foreign oppressors were called, and his political sympathies were racial rather than idealistic. Nor was his knowledge of the country to which we were bound very extensive; he had been there often as a courier and guide, but he had never lived there. He could add nothing essential to the information given to me by Don Gregorio.

My fund of knowledge amounted to this: The country of Roncador was one of the smallest of the former Spanish provinces. It consisted of a high upland plateau, about the same size as Ireland. It was entirely pastoral in character, and only its geographical frontiers preserved its economic and political identity. That identity would never have existed but for the activities of the Jesuits, who early in the seventeenth century had penetrated into this fertile district, established a mission there, converted and organised the Guarani Indians who had previously led a more or less nomadic existence, taught them the principles of agriculture and trading, and some of the mechanical arts, such as shoe-making, carpentry and building. For a hundred and fifty years they had guided the destinies of the community they had been instrumental in creating, and, though there is no doubt that they had exploited the Indians for the worldly glory of their priesthood, yet the system was designed for the general good, and if they had not made themselves objects of envy to the temporal powers, they might have succeeded in establishing a rational and truly Christian order of society which would have been an example to the whole world. But not content with supervising the spiritual and economic welfare of the communities they had founded, they sought to make themselves independent of the Spanish King, even in political matters (and, some say, of the Pope in theological matters). They carried their intrigues and pretensions to such a length that finally the King resolved to expel them from all his domains, and prepared his plans with such thoroughness and secrecy that in one night every Jesuit in the Spanish colonies was surprised and arrested by the civil and military authorities, sent to Buenos Ayres under escort, and from thence shipped off for Spain.

This event had taken place between sixty and seventy years before my arrival in America. The rule of the Jesuits had lasted for a century and a half, and though it had been stern, and had kept the Indians in strict subordination, it had been stable and efficient. After the expulsion of the Jesuits, the missions either fell into utter decay, the Indians reverting to their primitive mode of existence, or they fell, as was more often the case, into the hands of unscrupulous Spaniards and creoles. A Spanish governor and three lieutenants were appointed to each colony; to each town a civil administrator for temporal affairs and two curates for spiritual affairs. Actually such government was a cloak for a system of spoliation and robbery; it is reckoned that in the four years following the expulsion of the Jesuits the wealth of

most of the missions in cattle, horses and sheep declined
by more than half its former worth.

I was later to learn much more about the government
of the Jesuits, but for the moment I will not burden my
narrative with further facts. Sufficient to say that for the
past sixty odd years the colonies and missions had continued to decline in wealth, in population, and in all the
outward signs of civilisation. When at the break-up of
the Spanish empire the colonies had declared their independence, all the inhabitants looked forward to an improvement in their condition; and certainly, from the
point of view of the settlers and traders who had adopted
the country as their own, everything was to be gained by
the rejection of the Spanish dominion. The power fell
into the hands of the officers of the local militia (forces
formerly recruited by the Spanish garrisons), assisted in
some cases by a lawyer and a merchant or two. In most
cases a military dictatorship was established, but since
such governments had no purpose beyond the self-
aggrandisement of the dictator, they only served to
attract the cupidity of other potential dictators. Political
intrigues invariably ending in bloodshed were further
complicated by the action of the new priests, who, finding themselves in conflict with every dictatorship in turn,
did all in their power to impede administration. Meanwhile the unfortunate Indians found themselves worse
off than ever; not only did they lack the political organisation and arms to make a revolt possible; they were
even devoid of the necessary initiative. Utterly demoralised, they became the helpless victims of whoever possessed the authority to oppress them.

Against this system of oppression the Society of
Patriots in Buenos Ayres was endeavouring to set the
principles of the French Revolution. Their task was

hopeless, and destined to failure. For though they could convert the Indians, and though oppression had engendered the spirit of rebellion, yet the agents necessary to organise and lead such a popular movement were completely lacking. In the whole breadth of the continent there was scarcely a man of political inclinations whose conduct was above the suspicion of venality, and who was free to devote himself to the cause of the oppressed people. The committee in Buenos Ayres consisted for the most part of men attached by affairs and families to that city, and fully occupied with their own political future. It was for this reason that they had besought their comrades in Cadiz to send out approved agents, one of whom I had unwittingly become.

The efforts of such agents would have been quite futile but for the existence within most of the colonies of dissatisfied elements among the military forces. These forces, as I have already said, were not purely Spanish; in fact, if by Spanish is meant 'born in Spain,' the purely Spanish element, especially in the remoter colonies, was but a minority. At the time of the secession of the colonies many even of the purely Spanish elements had gone over to the service of the new government, and these formed the nucleus of the military dictatorships. Apart from these, the greater number of the soldiers consisted of men born in the colonies, generally of a Spanish father and an Indian mother. But there was no strict racial barrier, and even pure Indians were enrolled in the lower ranks.

There existed, therefore, the possibility of making a division between the Spanish-born and the American-born military elements. The former, who had nothing but their military bravado to recommend them, were often intolerable in their bearing, as well as idle and corrupt in their manners; the latter, with families and property in their vicinity, had interests beyond the barrack-room and parade-ground, and were consequently more sober in their behaviour and more sympathetic towards the natives. The possible strategy for a revolutionary party, therefore, was to enlist the aid of these more sympathetic elements in the army, and so to overcome the dictatorship by the very means by which it maintained itself.

You should realise that what I have dignified by the name of an army was often a force of a few hundred men, indifferently armed with old carbines. In exceptional cases they might possess one or two pieces of artillery. Naturally all the men were mounted, or mountable, for horses were everywhere plentiful. In Roncador the army consisted of four companies, each of something less than two hundred men. But the staff of officers was, as usual, out of all proportion to the size of the army, including five generals, a dozen colonels, and twenty or thirty officers of lower rank.

Such, so far as I can now recollect, was the extent of my knowledge before I came to Roncador. But it had already been established by the Society of Patriots that a sufficient support for a new government could be found, not only among the Indians, but even in the army, and secret negotiations had taken place between the committee in Buenos Ayres and Chrisanto Santos, the general to whom I was to report. Santos, although he had risen to the highest rank in the army, belonged to a family long established in the colonies, whose blood was not unmixed with that of the Indians with whom he sympathised. But though eager to change the existing state of things, and to establish order and justice in the place of chaos and oppression, there was no one of sufficient education or experience in the country with whom he could co-operate. He could, he felt, establish order, but he had no stomach for the details of political administration, without which it is impossible to govern a community.

When we had rested for twenty-four hours, we left for the last short but arduous stage of our journey. We hired four mules, and an extra man to act as guide. The path wound upwards through a rocky and precipitous valley, sometimes following the bed of the stream, sometimes climbing high above the banks across thickly wooded slopes. About midday we reached the summit of the pass, and there we rested four hours. Though we were at least four thousand feet above the sea level, the autumn day was still and warm. My gaucho and the guide slept in the shade; the mules were busy stamping their feet and twitching their hides to keep off the tiresome insects which infested them. I was now too excited to sleep, at once eager and apprehensive, on tiptoe, as it were, at the threshold of a country which held my destiny. The grassy track at my feet, the vista of wooded hills, the vast open sky above me, all invited me forward with a secret promise.

I roused my companions towards four o'clock, and even cursed them for their sluggishness. Our destination was only six miles away, and the descent of a thousand feet more gradual. But the woodland paths were often impeded with new undergrowth and fallen branches, so that it was nearly seven o'clock when we finally reached a clearing and saw before us a low estancia or farmhouse, built of wood and clay-filled wattles. We halted on the edge of the clearing whilst our guide went forward to warn the owner of our approach.

He presently came back, signalling us to approach.

The house did not differ much from many I had seen on my journey from the coast. It consisted of two long rooms, the first furnished with a table and a few rough chairs, the second with a couple of beds. An old man, his broad brown wrinkled face wreathed in silky white hair, came forward to greet us. This was Borja Yrabuyé, the Indian in whose cottage I was to await the instructions of General Santos. He spoke a little Spanish, and was infinitely polite, indeed servile. In an incredibly short time he had ready an excellent meal of roast beef and yucca root, followed by yerba tea and cigars. Afterwards I amused myself by attempting to talk with Yrabuyé in the Guarani dialect and before bedtime had made some progress.

The next morning the gaucho left early for Roncador, to warn General Santos of my arrival, and to receive instructions. Roncador (the principal town having the same name as the country) was a full day's ride away, so I could not expect Pedro's return for forty-eight hours. I sent the guide back with the mules, and spent the following two days in the excellent company of Yrabuyé, from whom, in spite of difficulties of communication, I learned much of the customs of the country, the state of affairs among the Indians, their complaints against the Spaniards and their desire for a settled government. Incidentally, I continued to improve my knowledge of the dialect.

Pedro did not return the evening of the second day of his absence, as I expected, but on the third day he reappeared, accompanied by General Santos himself. Of exceptionally low stature, the General made up for his physical deficiencies by a fiery but good-humoured appearance, the effect mainly of his dark restless eyes and a black beard, streaked with grey, which radiated from his face like the bristles of a sweep's brush. He talked rapidly and effusively, greeting me with such a torrent of words that I was relieved of the necessity of making any adequate response. Yrabuyé, who was a dependant of the General's, and had often accompanied him on shooting expeditions, soon welcomed his master with a meal to his liking, which we all shared. Afterwards the General and I drew apart and held a long interchange of views. I call it an interchange of views, but my part of the conversation was mostly in the form of questions, which General Santos answered without reserve. Actually he was old enough to be my father, but he treated me without the least condescension, attributing to me a political wisdom and wide experience of affairs which I assumed without protest. In dealing with men of action I have always found that in matters which they regard as intellectual they have no perception nor possibility of judgment, and will readily accept the most superficial display of knowledge as a profound mystery beyond their grasp, provided always that the display is made with calmness and confidence.

The General had let it be assumed that he had gone to the mountains for a day's shooting, so we had the whole of the following day to discuss and elaborate our plans. The General was of the opinion that surprise must be the principle of our strategy. Once the city was occupied, and the Spanish officers under arrest, we need fear no further opposition from the people of Roncador. We should, indeed, proclaim a popular government and invite their assent to the new constitution, a constitution which would follow the model indicated by the most enlightened philosophers of Europe.

The General could count on the fidelity of his own

company, but it would be difficult to assemble them without the knowledge of the other officers. Anything in the nature of a company parade, which I suggested, or a company field-day, was unknown to the Roncadoi army. The only parades indulged in took place on fes tival occasions, and then involved the whole army. There seemed to be no simple or straightforward solution of the problem. I then asked the General to give me some precise idea of the layout of the city and the land sur rounding it. The city was simplicity itself, consisting of a central square, from each corner of which two streets branched off at right angles. There were some minor streets or lanes intersecting these at irregular intervals. All was situated on the slopes and top of a semi circular mound (actually the escarpment of a plain) round the foot of which a river flowed. The river, itself of no considerable dimensions, ran through a stony bed, and was crossed by a single bridge of three arches span. The street to the bridge ran off from the north west corner of the square, and was the principal thoroughfare.

The town itself consisted for the most part of huts, except on the east side of the square. There, more than a hundred years ago, the Jesuits had constructed their cathedral, flanked by two lower stone buildings, one formerly the college of the Jesuits and now used as a barracks and military headquarters, the other a ware house and seat of the civil administration. The whole of the army staff occupied quarters in the college, which was built round a large quadrangle, with a covered cloister extending all the way round.

The only entrances to the cloisters were two: one direct from the square, a covered way capable of admit ting a cart, or four men abreast; the other from the north transept of the cathedral, a doorway of normal dimensions.

It is useless to describe the several alternative plans we elaborated during the day; most of the obvious ones were discarded owing to the nature of the human material at our command. Though he could trust his men to follow him in person whenever and wherever he led them, General Santos despaired of even communicating to them a secret plan of operations; nor could he answer for their reliability, because the very simplicity of their characters prevented many of them understanding the subtle nature of an intrigue, or the necessity of silence. We therefore finally dismissed any plan which involved mass action, and resolved on a swift operation employing very few men. Such action would have to be drastic and spectacular, and I, who had hitherto considered myself among the most humane and tender-hearted of men, found myself considering, and even urging, the method of assassination. Merely to arrest the Dictator and his immediate associates might provoke desperate opposition among the remaining officers; and however loyal our forces, and however favourable the populace, a victory would not be assured without a struggle involving untold bloodshed.

We decided that our plan should contemplate, in the first instance, the assassination of the Dictator alone; other executions would only be carried out if the event provoked definite opposition. But the General was fairly confident that the death of the Dictator would not be regretted even among his associates, for those who were not inspired by fear or personal antipathy were probably envious.

We decided next that the assassination should be spectacular. A private assassination would involve the further problem of publicity, the endless repetition of explanations; and explanations are only effective in such circumstances if accompanied by a display of force. This decision implied in effect that the assassination should take place in the square, at an hour when a considerable number of people would be about.

The assassination should be followed by the immediate declaration of a republic, the abolition of the military dictatorship, and the establishment of the rule of the people by free election of representatives.

So much determined, the problem resolved itself into settling on the most suitable occasion. The General, after some thought, recalled that on the first Sunday of April (which was late autumn in the latitude) there took place the ceremony of the presentation of the tithes. Originally introduced by the Jesuits, this method of supporting the clergy had been continued under the Spanish rule, but owing to the rivalry of Church and State which had then developed, it had become difficult for the priests to enforce this tribute. Recently, under the military dictatorship, the whole system had been revised, the tithes reduced to reasonable proportions, and their collection enforced by arms. To mark this new agreement between the Church and the Government, the Dictator had established the custom of attending in state the ceremony of blessing the tithes. By great good fortune, General Santos had been entrusted with the necessary arrangements for the military participation, this year as on former occasions. Our task seemed therefore to be enormously simplified.

It occurred to me then that we should be risking the success of the plot if in any way the assassination interfered with the ceremony in the cathedral, or if blood were shed in the immediate vicinity of a building held sacred by the people. It would be easy, for example, to plant assassins in the porch of the church, who would fall on the Dictator as he emerged at the head of the procession. We might even plant other men inside the church who, as soon as the shot was fired, would close the doors of the church and prevent the exit of the Dictator's bodyguard. Nothing could be neater than such a plan, but the General confirmed my fear that the deed might in that event distress the religious susceptibilities of the people, and end by making a martyr of the Dictator.

We did not make any further progress with our plans that day, but as there were still three weeks to elapse before the Sunday in question, it was decided that on the morrow I should accompany the General to his farm, which was situated about five miles to the west of the city. There we could elaborate the details of our plan of action carefully and patiently. That my presence at the farm might be noticed and reported in Roncador did not seem to the General to be a matter of great importance; he would never be suspected by his fellow-officers of harbouring a political agent, and among the people the knowledge of my existence, and perhaps the general diffusion of a certain atmosphere of wonder and mystery, would be to the advantage of our plans.

Accordingly the next day we were early in the saddle. I said farewell to the gentle Yrabuyé, and promised to return and shoot partridges with him before many weeks were past. My gaucho, who might at this stage have returned to Buenos Ayres, begged me to retain him as a body-servant in this country of savages, and, the General consenting, I willingly engaged him, for he was the image of fidelity.

The country we passed through was of a delicious

freshness. Green pastures alternated with groves of trees, and everywhere ran pleasant streams. The shrubs and trees were of great variety, many unknown to me; but I recognised the lime, the orange and the fig tree. Smaller plants, some of them fragrant, hung down from the branches of the larger trees, and in this aerial garden lived a whole world of creatures—squirrels, monkeys, parrots, and other birds of gorgeous plumage. But most attractive of all were the myriads of humming-birds which darted from tree to tree, or hovered suspended in the air about us. I had often seen these little creatures— some of them were no larger than insects—on my way up from the coast, but never in such quantities, nor in such dazzling variety. Some of them seemed actually to gleam like precious stones or bright metals, at once translucent and iridescent; their hues ran from cinnamon to crimson, purple, violet, indigo and green. In flight, their wings vibrate so quickly as to become invisible, and then they emit that low murmur which gives them their name. The General was pleased to see my delight in these 'angels,' as he called them, and explained that he loved them so much himself, that he had peopled his house with them.

Here and there the land became more marshy, and we passed one or two lakes, covered with ducks, water-hens and snipe. Partridge and quail ran about the grassy clearings. Sometimes among the trees I spied a white-washed cottage or farmhouse, and signs of cultivation were frequent—strips of cotton-plant, yucca, and tobacco-plant, and sometimes, near the farmhouses, a fenced field of Indian corn or sugar-cane. The inhabitants, such as we saw, were natives, living in extreme simplicity. At one cottage we stopped for water, which was brought to us in a rough earthenware jug by the master of the house. He stood uncovered while we drank, his wife and children standing respectfully in the background, their hands crossed over their bosoms. The General told me that this was their custom with all strangers, and was in no way a special tribute to him.

We rode easily and arrived at the General's farm about five o'clock in the evening. The country was now less wooded, but still fertile. Large herds of cattle and horses roamed about the open prairies. The farmhouse stood in the shelter of a group of trees—a long low building, with an open verandah. Our arrival was the signal for a great barking of dogs and fluttering of fowl. Young gauchos sprang from the shade to take our horses, and the General led me into his estancia. He lived here with a native wife and nine children, the eldest of whom was a young woman of twenty-two. He kissed them all in turn, and then introduced me as Doctor Olivero—a name we had agreed on as suitable for the country. We did not stay, however, with the family, but made our way to the General's own room, at one end of the house. Here I was introduced to the rest—the most numerous part—of the General's family: his humming-birds that lived in half a dozen cages hung round the walls of his room. There he fed them, and there they bred. He opened the cages and they flew out with shrill little cries, fluttering round the General, who had furnished himself with quills filled with syrup, into which the hovering birds dipped their tongues. Others flew about his ears, hovered round his mouth, buzzed and fluttered about his head and hands. When tired of playing with them, he put the quills away; and then he gently waved his hands in the midst of them, at which signal they all returned to their respective cages.

In an alcove I noticed a few books, but except for a

table and two chairs, there was no other furniture in the room. Almost the whole of one side was open to the verandah, from which the open landscape sloped into a distant view of wooded hills, suffused with the first golden flush of autumn, Here, on the verandah, as I was presently to discover, the whole family slept in hammocks. But before we had reached that restful stage our hunger had been satisfied by a well-cooked meal, served to us by the General's daughters.

The next day the General returned to Roncador, and left me to meditate among his books .and hummingbirds. It was long before I could establish any intimate relationship with the latter, for no doubt my lean features and tall figure, compared with the General's short and shaggy frame, had all the strangeness of a new species. Among the books I found several of a political nature, calculated to inspire a liberal and sympathetic outlook—among them Volney's great work. which had so much influenced my own youthful mind.

In these surroundings I spent three of the most pleasant weeks of my whole life. The climate was so bright and temperate, the life of the household so gay and simple, so devoid of ceremony or conventions of any kind. I rose early and bathed in a near stream; I spent the morning shooting wild ducks and partridges, or riding with one of the General's sons about the estate; I spent the long shaded siestas in the General's room; I read slowly and thoughtfully, refreshed occasionally by cups of yerba tea, my senses lulled by fragrant and freshly-made cigars. I found it very difficult to realise that I was the same being who a few years ago had been eating out his heart in an English village; who had lived through varied scenes in London, Warsaw and Cadiz.

My mind utterly refused to believe in the concurrent existence of such diverse places; my memory was a long thread, stained with these multi-coloured experiences, now coiled up in my brain. Beyond the present, no other reality could exist for me.

General Santos came home every few days, and sometimes stayed for two days at a time. We spent many hours in conference, elaborating our plans. Two developments were in our favour. The Dictator had difficulty in finding sufficient ready money to pay the army he kept mobilised, and a spirit of dissatisfaction was evident among them; and as the time for the paying of the tithes drew near, a section of the people were murmuring, as usual, against this imposition. Roncador did not differ from other countries in this respect, that the churches were filled with women and children, whilst the men, their days occupied by physical labour and their nights by necessary sleep, found little time, and indeed had little need, for the consolations of religion. This division was further accentuated by the priests and friars, who, to buttress their authority, sought every means of acquiring a dominating influence over the womenfolk.

As the day of action drew nearer, although we were in fuller command of all the factors in the situation, the inspiration for the actual stroke was lacking. I therefore resolved to accompany the General to Roncador, there to survey as closely as possible the actual spot chosen for the act of liberation. For this purpose I exchanged clothes with my gaucho, and rode in as the General's attendant. The General was to make some purchases in the market, and send me back with them. We arrived at the city without incident. I was interested to see how the reality of its situation compared with the mental image I had

formed from the General's description. The plan and
situation were not to be mistaken; it was all of such simplicity. But I had imagined a city of greater regularity
and more imposing appearance. Actually it was a pitiful
collection of huts and sheds, the sandy streets unpaved
and unclean. The streets sloping towards the river were
worn by rains and by water from open springs, and were
more like the bed of a ravine. The plaza or central square
presented a different appearance. The houses round three
sides of it, mostly belonging to merchants and shop-
keepers, were of larger dimensions, and generally two
storeys high. The ground floor was recessed, to form an
open arcade which ran round the square after the fashion
of a cloister. Here and there booths were erected on the
other side of this covered way. The open square, about
four acres of bare earth, was deserted when we arrived.
The most remarkable feature of the place, however, was
the eastern side of the square, occupied by the cathedral
and two other buildings—the barracks and the ayuntiamento, or the administrative offices. These three structures completely dwarfed the rest of the town. The
church was only to be judged by its façade, which was a
perversion of the baroque style, an enormous baldaquin
in stone and stucco, to which was attached a wooden
portico flanked by spirally twisted columns and sur-
mounted, in a niche which was a veritable crow's-nest of
fantastic metal ornament, by a life-sized figure of the
Virgin of the Assumption. A flight of about a dozen
wide steps led down to the level of the square. The other
two buildings, each two storeys high, were by contrast
severe and prison-like; built of roughly hewn granite,
their windows were defended by iron grilles.

We rode up to the building on the left of the cathedral
and, passing a sentry, entered the courtyard, where we

left our horses in the charge of the General's groom. It was the hour of the siesta, and there were few people about. I have already mentioned the door from this courtyard which gave access to the cathedral. Using this entrance, we made our way into the dark interior. The smell of dampness and decay was my first impression of the general ruin which I soon discovered everywhere about me. The roof was in places open to the sky, and long streaks of greenish stain trailed down the once whitewashed walls. The droppings of birds disfigured the cornices, the pillars, and even the saints whose statues presided over the melancholy scene. The high altar was stripped and obviously not in use, but in the side chapels a few candles were burning, and here and there an old woman was kneeling in prayer.

The General explained that for the Blessing of the Tithes the high altar would be temporarily refitted. The church would be filled with worshippers, the women on one side, the men on the other side separated by a wide aisle. Down this aisle would pass, first the Bishop and priests, the choristers, the neophytes, and the virgins bearing the symbolic fruits. The Dictator would follow with his staff and the officers of the city, the judges and magistrates. They would take their places in front of the people, and then the tithes would be blessed. The procession would then re-form, the priests proceeding to the sacristy, the secular officers and their followers going out by the great western porch, down the steps to the Square. In the Square the Dictator would review his miniature army, drawn up there in parade formation. Standing at the foot of the steps, he would take the salute as the troops marched past on their way to the barracks, and then he would follow them. Afterwards, various equestrian sports, including a *sortija* and a bull-fight, would be held in the Square—not the true Spanish bull-fight, but a scuffle of untrained Indian toreros and tame bulls.

I questioned the General closely about the procedure. Standing at the foot of the cathedral steps, where the Dictator himself would stand five days later, two thoughts occurred to me: 1, a dictator should never venture before his people on foot; 2, a dictator should never march at the rear of his army.

There was little more we could do in the way of sight-seeing without attracting undue attention, so when we had made some purchases we left the city, still somnolent in the evening sun. We were silent as we rode back, meditating on the desperate action now so near performance.

Slowly a plan was taking shape in my mind—a plan which appealed to me because it seemed to promise to possess the fantasy of a natural event. Man is always so clumsy and direct in his self-willed deeds; the knife, a bullet, poison—there is no play between the intention and the crude act. When the ancient gods wished to kill Æschylus, they sent an eagle into the sky, carrying a tortoise in its claws—an insecure and heavy burden, which presently slipping from its grasp, fell like a bolt through the air and crushed the skull of the aged poet. In such a way I would have liked to bring about the death of the Dictator.

My plan was to stage the assassination as part of the festivities. In the Square a circular palisading would be erected, a temporary ring to hold back the spectators. On the south side of the Square a special box would be fitted up for the Dictator and his friends. Though I had never seen a bull-fight, I was familiar enough with its procedure from the conversation of my fellow-prisoners in Cadiz, and the first plan I outlined to General Santos was this: that at some stage in the fight the torero should entice the bull towards the Dictator's box, incite it so that he was compelled to take sudden refuge in the box itself, and there plunge his sword into the Dictator instead of into the bull. The General commended my ingenuity, but raised these objections: he doubted whether there existed in Roncador an *espada* skilful enough to entice the bull in the required direction; and, moreover, by the time the fight had reached its final stage, the *suerte de matar*, the bull was generally too dazed and exhausted to spring forward in a manner sufficiently surprising to make a resort to the Dictator's box feasible.

I immediately saw the force of these objections, and turned my thoughts towards the other sport indulged in on such occasions. The *sortija* is a much simpler and more innocent amusement. A frame, like that of a door, and wide enough to allow a horse and rider to pass through it with ease, is erected in an open space. From the middle of the horizontal bar of the frame a ring is suspended by a slender cord. The horseman, taking his stand about two hundred yards away, gallops towards the frame at full speed and attempts to carry away the ring on the point of a dagger or spear. Usually a successful rider receives a great ovation, and at Roncador would prance round the arena, saluting the Dictator as he passed his box.

The frame would be erected in the middle of the Square, opposite the cathedral porch. The riders would take their stand at the north end, so that the Dictator would have a clear view of the event from his box, and would therefore, I perceived, be in the direct line of the onrushing horse. A rider could, before anyone realised what was happening, spur on his horse, leap the palisading, and there find a target less elusive than a suspended ring.

All that was lacking was a man daring enough and skilful enough to risk his life in this action.

At first General Santos distrusted the elaborate nature of my plan; he would honestly have preferred some straight shooting, but when I pointed out the immense psychological effect of such a swift and surprising blow, he was slowly convinced, and ended by adopting the idea with enthusiasm. That evening we discussed every aspect of the plan—every possible eventuality; and decided on the consequential steps to be taken. We agreed that as soon as the deed was accomplished, the barracks, the cathedral and the ayuntiamento should be occupied by armed men of the General's company; that a republic should be at once declared and a proclamation issued; that the Spanish officers should all be arrested and any resistance met by death.

Once our plan was settled, we acted with resolution and intensity. Five days only were left for the completion of all the necessary arrangements. I anticipated that the most difficult part would be the provision of the actual assassin, but the General assured me that he knew a dozen men who would welcome the opportunity of revenge—men who had been insulted or ill-treated by the military dictatorship. The General himself was most concerned for the details of the proclamation, but this I offered to draft within twenty-four hours, and draft it in such a way that all the classical dogmas of democratic government should be clearly embodied. The principles, I assured him, had long been settled by the Fathers of the Revolution (by which general title I designated such philosophers as Rousseau, Raynal and Volney); all that was necessary was to apply these universal principles to the particular case of Roncador.

The General submitted very humbly to my display of intellectual arrogance, and with a wave of his hands, the gesture with which he had dismissed his humming-birds, he turned to those animated companions of his, and began to feed them from the quills of syrup.

He left for Roncador at an early hour the next morning. The mental excitement of our last conversation had kept me long awake, and before I fell asleep the outlines of a new constitution seemed to be clear in my mind. But when I awoke I felt dull and heavy, and it was only after several cups of yerba tea, and frequent recourse to Rousseau and Volney, that my phrases began to take form once again. Then I wrote swiftly and clearly, and was able to spend the second day merely in reviewing and correcting the periods of our proclamation.

[Here follows a translation of the printed proclamation, found among Olivero's papers.

PROVISIONAL ORDINANCE OF GOVERNMENT

To be submitted to an Electoral Convention of the Republic of Roncador

Preamble

All men being endowed by Universal Providence with the same faculties, the same sensations, and the same needs, by this very fact it was intended by Providence that they should have a right to an equal share of the earth's bounty. Since the bounty is sufficient for all needs, it follows that all men can exist in equal liberty, each the master of his own destiny.

Equality and liberty are the essential attributes of man, two laws of his being, elements of his very nature. Men unite to cultivate the earth and live on its fruits, and for this purpose they enter into mutual contracts; for every service freely rendered a just share of wealth is given. Liberty and equality are guaranteed by justice, which is the principle of government in a society of free men.

Articles of Government

Article 1.—The province of Roncador is free and independent; its government is elective; its laws shall be published by the authority of a popular assembly, and administered without fear or favour.

Article 2.—The authority to govern in the name of the people shall be given for a term of three years to a council of three persons, elected by the vote of the whole people; it shall deal with all the affairs of the state, military, economic and administrative. There shall be a secretary (appointed by the Council) with power to act for any member of the Council in the case of his disability.

Article 3.—The province of Roncador adheres to the one Catholic religion; but the Church has authority in spiritual matters only. It will elect its own bishops and conduct the education and administration of its own priesthood. Its revenues shall be provided by the willing charity of the worshippers in each parish. All compulsory tithes are abolished.

Article 4.—Besides the usual attributes of government, the Council shall possess the following powers: 1, to provide all the civil and military forces; 2, to levy taxes; 3, to form treaties of amity and commerce; 4, to undertake public works; 5, to make regulations for buying and selling the produce of the country, both internally and externally.

Article 5.—Each month there shall be published a general account of the revenues, the expenditures, and the balance in the treasury. Every three months there shall be published a detailed account of the public revenues and expenditures.

Article 6.—The arrangement of the troops, the order of the promotions, plans of defence and everything that relates to military affairs, appertain to the commander-in-chief, who shall be one of the three members of the Council.

Article 7.—Every male above the age of sixteen shall be ready to defend his country when required.

Article 8.—Justice shall be administered by a court of judges, who shall be paid a fixed salary by the State, but shall be otherwise independent of all political control, being appointed by their own college, and removed by a petition of the people. In each parish there shall be a justice of the peace, appointed by the bench of judges and answerable to them for the administration of local justice.

Article 9.—In each town or district there shall be a mayor, elected by the people, and responsible for the local administration of economic affairs. The mayor may, if the people so wish it, be a justice of the peace, but whilst a justice of the peace holds office at the pleasure of the bench of judges, a mayor is elected by the people for a term of two years.

Article 10.—The electors consist of every married man, and of widows who act as head of a household. The priests shall not vote, nor in any way take part in political or judicial affairs.

Article 11.—All commerce with other countries shall

be conducted under the supervision of the government.

Article 12.—The practice of usury is abolished.

This constitution is proclaimed by the provisional government of General Santos. He has appointed as Secretary to the provincial government the illustrious Doctor Olivero, recently arrived from that classic land of liberty, England, and learned in her universally admired laws and institutions. The provisional government will be submitted to the approval of the people at a general assembly to be held this day four weeks hence.

Dated at Roncador, 1st May, 183–.]

After an absence of thirty-six hours, General Santos returned for an evening and a night. His plans had met with every success. That is to say, under the guise of making the usual arrangements for the festival, he had interviewed twelve men of his company, creoles or Indians, who had all, upon being sworn to secrecy, professed a willingness to carry out any commands the General might give them. To each of these men he had separately revealed our intention to proclaim a republic on the following Sunday, and he had brought them together and asked them to select from the roll of the Company the names of as many companions as they each could rely on in the event of necessity. To these companions they were not to reveal our plan, but on the morning of the Festival each group was to be persuaded to meet on the east side of the Square to watch the sports. The General himself, as officer in charge of the festivities, would be on duty and mounted. The leader of each group should keep a close watch, for at a given moment he proposed to draw his sword and lift it above his head. At this signal they should all withdraw to the guardroom of the barracks and arm themselves. They should immediately reappear on the Square, where he would take charge of them and direct further operations.

To a query I raised, the General replied that the guard on duty at the barracks would be supplied by his own Company, and would offer no resistance to their friends.

He proposed to give the signal immediately the assassin had set out on his fatal ride. The few seconds that would elapse would not be sufficient for the concerted movement to be noticed before the deed had been accomplished, especially as the general attention would be on the rider; and it was essential to set the movement going before the deed had been accomplished, because otherwise the sudden general confusion might distract the soldiers from their purpose.

For the assassin the General had selected an Indian named Iturbide, who had recently been degraded by the Dictator. This man's magnificent physique and his skill on horseback had formerly made him a favourite with the officers, and he had actually been given the rank of lieutenant. Some of the Spanish officers, resenting the presence of a native among their ranks, had induced him under the influence of wine to make bold and incautious comments on the Dictator's personal conduct, and had then reported these remarks to the Dictator himself. Furious at the thought that anyone to whom he had shown special favour should thus abuse his position, the Dictator without further enquiry had ordered a parade of the whole army, and had then publicly stripped off the lieutenant's badges of rank. Dismissed from the army, Iturbide had sunk into abject beggary and despair, in which condition he thought only of revenging himself for this unjust humiliation.

To treat openly with such a man would have been an extreme risk. Nor was he easily accessible through any of the men in the Company, for in becoming an officer Iturbide had forfeited his social integrity, and his disgrace had not been of a nature to reinstate him in the regard of his companions. The man was therefore a social outcast, though still respected by the civilian youth of the place for his strength and ingenuity. Santos, however, had sent his groom to seek out Iturbide, and persuaded him to be on the bridge when they passed on their way back to the farm. Knowing that the General had always been sympathetic towards him, Iturbide had readily agreed to the rendezvous. There they had met this very morning, and Iturbide had taken the groom's horse and ridden by the General's side. The plan was unfolded to him, and step by step the Indian pledged himself to secrecy, and finally to his own implication in the plot. The General, on his part, had promised him full protection after the execution of the deed, and the rank of Captain in the republican army. Other details, such as the provision of a horse and a tilting spear, had also been arranged, and Iturbide had then returned quickly to the city.

We reviewed our plan of operations until late in the night. We covered many possible eventualities which I cannot now recollect, but on only one point did we feel at a loss. We could imagine no means of having our proclamation printed in advance of the event. There existed only one printing press in the whole of Roncador, and this was subservient to the Dictator's government. Our despair might have led us to a modification of our plans had not General Santos observed, late in the night, that not one citizen in a thousand could read a proclamation even if it were printed, and that therefore we might as well not print it at all, but have it proclaimed in a loud voice.

With the terms of the proclamation which I had drafted the General professed himself perfectly satisfied. He only doubted whether the Indians would understand a word of the preamble; he admitted, however, that eloquence was an essential instrument of government, and therefore allowed me to retain my phrases. The actual details of the constitution he found admirably adapted to the country and its people, and he was obviously impressed by my grasp of political affairs. Since I had been sent to him in such a capacity, I allowed this impression to remain undisturbed by any modest protestations.

The time that was left to us was spent by me in a state of affected calmness; I was silent and to all appearance bemused, but I felt that the impetuous beating of my heart was only restrained by an effort of my will. I made several copies of the proclamation, but otherwise I could do nothing but wait. General Santos was kept in Roncador, but he returned on the eve of the Festival. All was in train. He had made certain more detailed provisions, and certain men had been given definite stations in the barracks and the cathedral. All else must wait on the event.

The next day I left the farm early in the morning to be present at the ceremony of the Blessing of the Tithes. The dilapidated church had been decorated with a few tawdry banners, and the high altar was set out with bright vessels and lighted candles. The nave was filled with a crowd of country people, timid and pious in their demeanour. The ritual I have already described; it was carried out in a perfunctory and hasty manner; the singing was execrable and the whole atmosphere listless. I took my place in the dark shadow behind the shaft of light that entered the main porch, and was interested chiefly to see the features of the man whose life was so soon to be forfeited. Presently I heard the regular tramping of feet and a harsh command. The march was halted, and then there entered, without music, a tall and solid figure, dressed in the uniform of a general. He was followed by five or six other officers, among whom was my friend Santos. When the service was finished I had a better opportunity to observe the Dictator, for he came directly towards the open doors, his face full in the brilliant light—a face so heavy and dull, so devoid of gentleness and intelligence, that I looked on it without pity.

The Dictator stayed on the steps of the cathedral and there received a salute from the four companies—that is to say, the whole army—which were drawn up in parade formation inside the improvised bull-ring, still unenclosed on the side towards the cathedral. A bugle-call then pierced the expectant air, there was a roll of drums, followed by the usual words of command. The companies formed into column of march, wheeled round the ring, passed the Dictator, who again took their separate salutes, and so filed into the barracks. The Dictator and his staff were left alone on the steps; they abandoned their formal attitudes and walked leisurely away to the ayuntiamento, where refreshments were waiting for them.

Meanwhile the ring was closed in and preparations made for the bull-fight. This was due to begin at eleven o'clock, and people began immediately to file into the benches. They were dressed in all kinds of antique finery, and the scene was soon very animated. Myself, I had resolved to stay on the cathedral steps, where I could obtain some shade from the fierce sun, and where the whole proceedings would be perfectly visible.

About a quarter-past the hour the Dictator and his staff emerged again. There were no cries of "Viva," no demonstration of any kind. Two soldiers guarded the box reserved for the Dictator's party, which was entered from behind, at the south end of the Square.

None of the bright ritual which accompanies a bull-fight in Spain was practised at Roncador. The espadas were clad in their ordinary riding-costumes, and a poncho, or everyday cloak, served as a muleta. A young bull was driven into the ring from a pen in the north-west corner of the Square; a picador on horseback appeared from the opposite corner. The bull was hardly to be tempted into action; only when goaded by the banderilleros did it display any anger. But in its timid hesitations and frustrated assaults it provided the spectators with sufficient cause for excited cries of execration and delight.

In spite of the general air of excitement, this part of the day seemed to me, and perhaps to everyone engaged in the conspiracy, to drag on interminably. In reality it did not last an hour, during which time three bulls were dispatched. It was now midday, and I began to fear that the rest of the sports would be abandoned. But the people of Roncador have little sense of the passage of time, and in any case the *sortija* was far too popular a contest to suffer such a fate. The last bull had not yet been dragged off the ring before men were erecting the framework in front of where I stood, whilst to the right the mounted contestants gathered in order of entry. I was at a disadvantage in that I did not know which figure was Iturbide There were about a dozen entrants, and their appearance was so various as not to lend particular distinction to any one of them.

It was perhaps ten minutes before the course was

ready. An incessant level chattering rose from the assembled spectators, pierced by the sudden cries of children, the shrill laughter of women, and above, in the high clear sky, the swerving scream of swallows. The heat of the sun sent up the smell of dust, sweat and blood. The sleek horses pawed the ground and pranced impatiently under their riders. I looked towards the Dictator's box. It was in the shade, a calm oasis; a group of four or five people smoking cigars, hatless, their swords stiffly projecting from their huddled bodies, the Dictator himself bulky in the middle of them. I looked round the Square, and noticed Santos seated on his horse, at the side of the other horses, but a little apart.

Then the men fixing up the frame picked up their spades and mallets and ran out of the ring. A trumpet was blown and the chatter and the cries of the crowd died down. Only the swallows continued to scream.

The first rider came galloping down the ring, his body pitched forward, his lance levelled past the horse's head. He thundered through the frame, but left the ring oscillating behind him.

Another rider came and then another. The third horse stumbled and pitched its rider, and was led ignominiously off. In the pause, whilst all eyes were occupied by this lucky accident, I noticed a movement among the soldiers standing on my side of the ring. They were gathering, trickling casually together. No one else would notice. Santos had taken advantage of the interruption to raise his sword.

Iturbide's horse was restless, rearing on its hind legs. Flakes of lathery foam flew off from its mouth. Then it was suddenly quiet and lurched forward. Its flanks rippled like silk in the sunlight.

Horse and rider crashed through the frame, the ring

swinging idly behind them. But on they went unswerv-
ingly, swift, swift; till there was an indrawn cry, a confused rising of men. The body of the rider was very low,
one with the horse and its lashing hooves.

A flash of sunlight caught the point of the lance. The
horse upreared, high against the palisading. Then there
was a downward lunge.

Men fell together in confusion, uttering aimless and
astonished cries. People were running across the ring
from all sides.

Behind, unobserved, Santos and his soldiers were
already emerging from the barracks, armed, in order.

From the confusion the horse emerged, unattended,
riderless.

The cry now, out of the confusion. The cry taking
shape, sounds becoming articulate. 'The Dictator! The
Dictator! The Dictator is dead!'

The crowd swayed, its outer rim broke. Three figures
emerged—two soldiers with Iturbide between them.
Iturbide was alive.

The crowd swarmed round them, crying out, questioning. Excited voices, burying everything in their confusion.

Then above it all a blare of trumpets, an order ringing
out clear.

The crowd turned towards the new diversion, saw the
armed men facing them, a solid phalanx. In front of
them, a General mounted. General Santos.

'To your homes. On pain of death, to your homes,'
the General cried. The order was taken up and cried
across the whole Square.

At the same time a detachment of soldiers was march-
ing past the cathedral towards the south end of the ring.
The crowd gave way before them as they advanced to-

wards the Dictator's box. Here they found the Spanish
officers, some bending over the mortally wounded Dictator, others arguing excitedly about the event. Arrived
before these officers, the squad halted and brought their
rifles to the ready position. The corporal in charge called
upon the officers to surrender their swords and return to
the barracks under escort.

Confused by the assassination of the Dictator, without
any resource in the emergency, the officers thus addressed
prepared to obey the order without protest. At that
moment General Santos rode up to the group.

'Gentlemen,' he said, addressing the Spanish officers,
'in the name of the people of Roncador I have assumed
command of the army of the Republic. The deed you
have just witnessed is an act of justice, rendered necessary by tyranny and oppression. Henceforth the people
of this land propose to govern themselves in liberty and
equality, freed for ever from the yoke of military dictators. Gentlemen, you are under arrest. You shall come
before a tribunal without delay, and your fate will there
be decided with justice and clemency.'

The astonished officers were not given a chance to
protest. At a word from the General the detachment
surrounded the officers, and the order was given to
march. The equally astonished people, who had retreated like startled jackals to the shelter of their
verandahs, looked out and saw the men who had for so
long terrorised them led like criminals towards the
barracks.

Guards had meanwhile taken up their positions at all
important stations. The arena was empty, except for the
body of the Dictator, which lay on the ground beyond
the broken palisading. General Santos now rode into the
middle of the arena, and cried out in a loud voice:

'The people of Roncador are henceforth free. The tyranny is at an end. Long live the republic!'

But such as heard him were too dazed by the events to respond. The General turned his horse and rode back towards the barracks. As he passed the cathedral steps he saw me standing there, and summoned me to follow him.

My first business was to attend to the printing of the proclamation. The printing press was immediately requisitioned, and by evening a large number of sheets were printed and freely distributed. Meanwhile the chief representatives of the law, certain magistrates and aldermen, were summoned to the barracks and asked to swear fealty to the provisional government. Without exception, everyone welcomed the new dispensation. It was decided to have the body of the Dictator buried immediately, and without any kind of public ceremony. Two friars were instructed to carry out the necessary arrangements. Finally, the treasurer of the Dictator's government was summoned before us and asked to present an account of the state's finances. All moneys in his possession, and found among the effects of the Dictator, were confiscated, and late that evening a month's wages were issued to the troops.

We worked continuously all that day, but towards dark we relaxed our efforts and had food brought to the headquarters we had established in the barracks. From time to time messengers came in to report the reception of the event among the people. After the first amazement there was general rejoicing, and late that evening, when a majority of the soldiers had been dismissed, there was great gaiety in the Square, the people dancing and singing until long past midnight.

Thus the revolution was accomplished. It lacked many

of the usual features of a revolution. There was only one
death, that of the tyrant, a death which, so far as we
knew, none regretted. There were no extraordinary
demonstrations of joy. The dancing that went on in the
Square was such as would in any case have taken place
at the conclusion of a festival. There was no popular
hero. General Santos had remained scrupulously modest
in his demeanour, and the actual assassin, Iturbide, was
satisfied to have escaped with his life. He did not even
seek out his companions, but at the General's invitation
stayed in the orderly-room, content to be a passive
witness to the results of his decisive act.

We all slept in the barracks that night. The next day
the business of reviewing the personnel of government
and appointing provisional military and civil officers was
rapidly concluded. I was nominated secretary to the
government and given an office with sleeping quarters,
both within the barracks. Beyond the conduct of immediate affairs, little could be done until a general assembly
had given their approval to the articles of the ordinance
of government, as set forth in the proclamation; and had
elected a governing council. The payment of tithes, however, was suspended, an unauthorised act bitterly resented by the Bishop. This ecclesiastic was early in conference with General Santos, but his protests were without avail; everything, he was told, would be submitted
to the judgment of the people or their representatives.
The Bishop, who was utterly devoid of the dignity
usually associated with persons holding his rank, poured
scorn on our liberal principles, and told us that the
people were too simple and ignorant to be capable of
self-government, that they were children who must be
taught obedience to their masters, who without compul-
sion would lapse into the savagery from which the

Church had rescued them. To this the General answered that he was determined the people should have the government they desired, even if it meant their ultimate ruin; but in his opinion that fate was not to be expected, for the people were by nature peaceful and reasonably industrious, and if protected from the exploitation of envious foreigners, would live in contentment.

General Santos asked me to make a review of the economic resources of the country, to draw up proposals for revenue and a budget of expenditure, and to estimate the minimum number and the nature of public offices required for the conduct of the nation's affairs. All my conclusions should be reduced to a simple form, capable of being presented to an assembly of the people's representatives.

Messengers were sent to every village and district, inviting them to send a delegate to the conference announced in the proclamation. Arrangements for the accommodation of these caciques, as they were called, who would probably arrive with their wives and children, were made in the city. Most of them would have to camp in the open square, or in the river valley and the slopes leading down to it.

I shall pass over the detailed history of this provisional period. I found myself involved in an ever-increasing multiplicity of functions, for nobody yet pretended to authority, and in such circumstances the decision is invariably left to the chief executive officer. Somewhat to my own surprise, I found myself enjoying the duties that devolved upon me. There is no joy comparable to the joy of government, especially in circumstances of virgin chaos. Not only inanimate things—money, equipment, goods of every kind—but even human beings, are so much plastic material for creative design. A sense of order is the principle of government as well as of art, and I found myself applying to my task all those instincts and ambitions which had been inhibited by my precipitate flight from England. I began to wonder whether all great administrators—a Solon, a Cæsar, a Charlemagne, a Napoleon—were not at bottom artists seeking a mode of expression. Certainly there is a profound difference between the man of action whose only end is action, a self-indulgent exercise of powerful muscles, and the man of action who moves towards some intellectual notion of order. There is also the man of action who only moves as the immediate circumstances dictate, jumping from one floating island to another as he is borne down the rapids.

My first business was to estimate the economic resources of the country. The area of Roncador was computed to be some 30,000 square miles, but the boundaries to the north and east were somewhat indefinite. In spite of its considerable area, the population was very sparse; apart from the uninhabited mountain ranges which formed its borders on the east and west, the central plains or pampas supported little human life. The villages were confined to the river basin; many streams had their source in the western ranges, spread over the marshy region in the north, and then gathered together as they turned south under the eastern watershed, eventually to join the powerful river which formed the southern boundary of the state. Under the Spanish rule, the province had been divided for administrative purposes into thirty districts, many of them not containing even the semblance of a village. Roncador itself was the only town of any size. The census I immediately had made revealed a population of 754 families, 3,064 souls, possessing an aggregate of 4,632 tame cattle, 1,780 oxen,

1,510 horses, 3,791 mares, 501 mules, 198 asses, 4,648 sheep and a few goats. After numerous enquiries, I computed the whole population of the state as about 14,000 families, totalling between 50,000 and 60,000 souls, with tame cattle in proportion, and wild cattle innumerable.

The country was entirely agricultural, and almost entirely self-supporting. This naturally simplified the problem of government. The only necessary imports were salt, carbines and uniforms for the army, paper, various tools and instruments, and a miscellaneous quantity of things which might be described as articles of luxury. The exports consisted of hides, yerba maté, sugar and tobacco, and were more than sufficient to balance the value of the imports. I at once decided that the simplest policy would be one which kept the inhabitants of the country content with an agricultural status, which held in strict control the mercantile exploitation of their products, and which so far as possible met the expenses of government from the surplus of export production. In other words, the imports might be taxed up to the limit of the value of the exports. Luckily I was not under the necessity of considering an adverse balance of exchange, and was of the opinion that such an eventuality should not be allowed to arise, even if it meant the exclusion of Roncador from all commerce with the outer world.

The administration of an economic policy presented no difficulties, since all buying and selling was done in the city of Roncador, and virtually the only exit for commerce was by way of the pass which circumvented the rapids already mentioned. The river itself was the only highway for commerce.

Whilst I cogitated these matters, General Santos reviewed the personnel of the administration. All pure

Spaniards were incontinently dismissed, and given one month to wind up their affairs and depart from the country. But such as were married to native women were allowed to stay, on condition that they took an oath of fealty to the new government, and undertook to devote themselves to private enterprise, preferably farming. The same proposal was made to the Spanish military officers, but they were not given their liberty until after the convention.

This took place on the appointed day. For two days before the caciques and their families were riding in from all points of the compass. Altogether about a hundred families arrived, and were accommodated in the manner described. The convention itself was held in the cathedral. It was a motley assembly. For the most part the delegates were clad in a jacket of white dimity, very short, and exceedingly tight; a bespangled waistcoat, still shorter than the jacket; knee-breeches of crimson velveteen, with highly-embroidered drawers hanging down to the ankle; a blue silk sash; potro-boots open at the toes; large silver spurs on the heels; a very small hat of hide half-covering the head, from under which hung a long queue of plaited black hair. Few of them could read or write, and fewer still understood the questions which they were called upon to decide. But two things were very clear to them: the difference between a Spaniard and an Indian, and the incidence of all tithes and taxes.

Most of them sat on the floor or lounged against the pillars and walls. They treated the sacred building with scant ceremony, smoking, spitting and talking freely. A dais had been erected in the transept, and punctually at the hour announced the *de facto* government entered through the cloister doorway and took their places on this platform. Besides Santos and myself, there appeared the remainder of the non-Spanish officers, including Iturbide, now once more restored to his commission and raised to the rank of captain, and the chief cacique or mayor of the city of Roncador. For the Council of Three laid down in the provisional ordinance, it had been agreed to propose, in addition to General Santos, Pasquál Arapatî, the owner of one of the largest estancias near Roncador, and Hermanegildo Chora, a retired judge. Our difficulty had been to find men of sufficient eminence, with time to devote to the affairs of government, who were not in any way compromised by Spanish nationality or professional interests. We particularly wished to exclude the mercantile interests, who were in any case of no numerical strength, and that more considerable body of lawyers which, by reason of its claim to superiority in education, might in time usurp the authority we had wrested from the military party.

The proceedings were simple. In my capacity as clerk to the Council I first of all recited the Proclamation, and then announced that in accordance with its provisions the assembly had been called together for the purpose of electing a governing council. Three citizens of distinction, men renowned for their honesty and patriotism, had agreed to submit their names to the approval of the assembly, but it would be in order for the assembly to suggest alternative names, in which case a vote would be taken.

I finished my statement and looked up at my audience. Not a soul moved; none ventured to speak. I held the silence for perhaps two minutes, and then raising my voice to its most impressive pitch, cried:

'Patriots of the free province of Roncador, assembled here in the name of the people, is it your will that for a period of three years you should be governed by your faithful servants, the General Chrisanto Santos, Don Pasqual Arapatî and Don Hermanegildo Chora? If yes, cry yes!'

That answer came sharp and spontaneous, some crying out in Spanish, others in their dialects, but all signifying their assent.

'Furthermore, is it your will that I, Don Olivero, delegate of the Society of Patriots, should act as Secretary to the Supreme Council?"

Again they assented, and our revolution was thus legalised. General Santos rose to speak, and spoke simply and well. He described how once the country of Roncador had been a peaceful and fruitful land, cultivated by an American people; how centuries ago the Spaniards had come and brought this people into subjection; how this tyranny had given place to the tyranny of unscrupulous and predatory dictators; how the people had groaned under this oppression; how their possessions had dwindled and their homes decayed. He then spoke of the new spirit of liberty and equality, which, born in Europe and there becoming established in every land, had now spread to America; in every province the dominion of Old Spain was at an end, and the people themselves, those who were born in the land, had now determined to be the guardians of their own destinies, to live in peace with each other and enjoy the bounty of the earth in common happiness.

General Santos's speech concluded the proceedings. A festival lasting until the end of the following day was declared. By evening flares were lit in the square, and to the music of three or four guitarreros the caciques and their wives and daughters danced with the citizens of Roncador. Another *corrida* was held, and this time six bulls were slain; the *sortija* which followed was without fatal consequences.

In a few days' time the last visitor had left, and a stranger then arriving in Roncador would have found it difficult to realise that the peaceful life of the place had ever been disturbed. Here, he would have said, is a civilisation, not elevated among the civilisations of the world, but founded on two eternal principles: the dignity of work and the fear of God.

But I, in my office, had no grounds for such complacency. General Santos had returned to his humming-birds, Arapatî to the cares of his estancia, and Judge Chora to the shade of his verandah. Iturbide had been made chief staff officer, or adjutant, and on him I could count for the conduct of military routine, whilst I applied myself to the problems of economics and administration.

To tell the truth, I did not meet with any practical difficulties. Salt was made a government monopoly, and promised to provide a steady and substantial revenue. The taxes on imports were first fixed at thirty per cent. *ad valorem*, but within three months this was reduced to twenty per cent. It would be wearisome to recount all the acts of administration which I devised, and to which the Council gave their willing consent. Under their operation prosperity quickly returned to the country and the people lived in great contentment.

Much more difficult to determine were the principles of government. If the inhabitant of Roncador had been a purely rational being, dependent for his happiness on his material prosperity, an efficient administration would have provided for all his needs. Ideally his spiritual well-being should have been the sole care of the Church, and the articles of the Constitution had been drawn up in this sense. But the Church as it existed was not so much corrupt as thoroughly decayed. The priests and friars were men of little education, in no way removed in their manners and morals from the bulk of their congregations. The head of the Church, the Bishop Andres Velasco, was old and now apathetic. Since the secession of the colonies from the mother country, communications with the sovereign Pontiff of Rome had almost ceased.

In this aspect of affairs I received no help from the members of the Council. Though all three were upright men, professing the Catholic faith, they utterly despised the clergy, both secular and regular. The friars especially were distrusted, not only because of the open profligacy of their lives, but also because of the undue influence they exercised on the people. The people of Roncador were simple-minded, and carried over into their Christianity the superstitious force of a primitive religion. A paî or holy father they reverenced as the immediate representative of God; they blindly followed the simple instructions given to them, and did whatever was required with willing hearts. Many of the more licentious members of the brotherhood took advantage of this superstitious confidence placed in them by the people, not only to feed their own moral depravity, but to create a general atmosphere of espionage and intrigue, from which they continually profited. Apart from authorising me to prepare measures to destroy the power of these conventicles, and to reform the hierarchical government of the Church, the Council remained indifferent to the problems involved; they were content to legislate from day to day in the light of the immediate circumstances.

My plans for a more enlightened policy would have taken much longer to formulate but for the acquaintance I soon made with a certain Paî Lorenzo. I had made enquiries for any books of the history of the Church in South America, and one night this friar, who was attached to the cathedral in some capacity resembling that of a sacristan, paid me a visit, bringing with him a manuscript work which he thought might interest me. It was entitled *Memoria sobra las Misiones*, and was in effect an account of the Jesuit colonies and missions written a few years after their expulsion from the country. Paî Lorenzo was in appearance no better than the rest of the friars; he was, moreover, fat in figure and dirty in dress. But there were signs of intelligence in his broad and bland features, and his gaze was straight and honest. I discovered that he had a lazy and somewhat cynical mind, but that he was interested in questions of history and had a fair knowledge of profane literature. He commended the manuscript to me, saying that he had found it full of interest, and a corrective of the traditional view of the Jesuit missions.

During the next few days I followed his advice, reading the clear Spanish writing without difficulty. My previous knowledge of the Jesuits did not go beyond mere generalities—I knew that they were a society founded in the sixteenth century by a Spaniard, Ignatius Loyola, with the express purpose of evangelising the heathen. I knew that the members of the society submitted to a rigorous education and discipline. I knew that their emissaries had penetrated into the remotest countries of Asia, Africa and America, and that in America they had converted many tribes of wandering Indians, to whom they represented themselves as descendants of St. Thomas, come with a message of eternal peace and happiness to the Indian race. I knew that in America, as in many other parts of the world, they had acquired great wealth and extensive powers; that they

had interfered freely in political affairs, and had finally
so provoked the resentment, and perhaps the jealousy, of
the secular powers, that they had been expelled, the
sovereign Pontiff himself concurring.

I now discovered that their system of government and
their general policy had been of a kind far exceeding in
idealism and disinterestedness any other kind of rule
which the unhappy Indians had experienced. I discovered
that they came to a country whose peaceful natives were
at the mercy of marauding bands of Portuguese settlers,
who by fire and sword had spread terror over all the
land; that in spite of these perils they preached to the
Indians, established them in colonies, instructed them in
agriculture and the mechanical arts, as well as in the art
of self-defence. Time and again these colonies were raided
and destroyed, but there were always new Jesuits ready
to replace those who had perished, gather together the
scattered remnants of the missions, and begin again the
task of colonisation.

In founding these colonies, the Jesuits acted upon the
principle that they were a body distinct from either the
civil or ecclesiastical powers of the community. Naturally, they professed allegiance to the Pope as their
spiritual father, and to the King, who ruled by divine
right; but in practice their institutions were completely
independent of all external authority, a paradoxical position which could only be maintained in the remote
regions where their colonies were founded.

The discipline of the Society within its own orders was
unfaltering. They were governed by a superior who had
his residence at Candelaria, a central point from which
he could readily visit the other establishments. This
superior had two lieutenants who lived, one on the banks
of the Paraná, and the other on the Uruguay. In addi-

tion to these functionaries, who conducted the more important business of the community, each town or colony had its curate, assisted by one or more priests according to its extent and population. One curate was responsible for the spiritual well-being of the community, ministered at the altar, and taught scanty elements of reading and writing. Another attended to temporal affairs, superintending the development of agriculture and the teaching of mechanical arts.

The Indians were instructed in the art of self-government. They had their mayor, judges and aldermen, who conducted courts and councils; but naturally a people so innocent of political traditions would be dependent to a great extent on the advice of the curates, to whom they deferred their authority. The Jesuits insisted above all upon the principle of absolute equality, in social station, in hours of work, and even in matters of dress. Those elected to offices were expected to set a good example to those not so honoured, and apparently earned nothing by way of reward beyond the respect of their fellows.

In economic matters the establishments were conducted upon the principle of community of goods. The herds of cattle and horses were the common property of the people; all agricultural produce was equally shared, or stored for common use. The profits of any sales were put into 'the fund of the community,' to be used for the building and adorning of their churches, and for the provision of common services, such as a hospital for the sick and a school.

Within this egalitarian community the curates no doubt exercised an autocratic power. They insisted on regular attendance at mass and maintained the strictest moral discipline. They even took steps to correct the conjugal apathy of the Indians. At various hours during the night they caused drums to be beaten in the villages; for the Indians, not lustful by nature and preferring, after a day's work in the fields, the bliss of sleep above all other pleasures, had to be awakened in this manner to a sense of their marital responsibilities.

There can be no doubt that in the course of two centuries the Jesuits accumulated considerable wealth in South America, in lands, in herds of livestock, and in gold and silver vessels. As a result of this wealth they became a power too obvious and extensive to escape the jealousy of the civil and ecclesiastical authorities, who were directed from Europe and who in any case regarded the colonies as legitimate sources of plunder. The story of the expulsion of the Jesuits is common history. The consequences for the Indians were disastrous. They once more became victims of spoliation, robbery and maladministration; their numbers and possessions decreased rapidly, and they gradually sank into a state of poverty and indifference. For many years they resented the priests and friars sent to replace the Jesuit brothers, and were quite unable to understand the system of dual authority forced upon them. They had been accustomed to the single authority of the Society, which through its curates directed both spiritual and temporal affairs. Now they were asked to accept the authority of a priest in one sphere, and that of a layman in the other; and since these individuals represented a continuous conflict of interests, the Indians were left in a state of hopeless confusion. The priests might want them, for example, to attend mass at a prescribed hour, which hour might be inconvenient for the lay administrator. Neither authority would give way, with the result that the poor Indians suffered punishment whatever they did.

Reduced to poverty or slavery by economic exploitation, thoroughly demoralised by indecisive government, dwindling by natural propensities, the original colonies or missions founded by the Jesuits gradually disappeared. The whole country would probably have drifted back to some form of barbarism but for the rise of the creoles. Despised by their blood relatives, the Spaniards, they were gradually made race-conscious by this antagonism, and eventually aspired to the control of the land of their birth. They became advocates of liberty and emancipation, in opposition to the Spanish dominion. Without their aid, as was already so obvious to me in Roncador, the formation of independent republics would never have been possible.

From my study of Paî Lorenzo's manuscript I was led to several convictions which remained with me all through my life in Roncador. It is possible that the picture of the Jesuit colonies given by the unknown chronicler was too favourable. It is possible, too, that I read into his bare descriptions a conception of society already latent in my mind. Not many years before I had read Plato's *Republic* with extraordinary enthusiasm; unconsciously I may have imagined the Jesuit colonies as a fulfilment of the ideals I then acquired. But only the conjunction of theory and history, and the possibility of action in those particular circumstances, could have given rise to the spirit of determination which from that moment was born in me.

I saw clearly that a stable government would only be possible given certain conditions which I began to formulate to myself in precise phrases. *Authority must be single.* By single I did not mean necessarily resident in one person; the Jesuits, it is true, ultimately relied on the single authority of the Superior of their Society, but the government of each colony was entrusted to two curates, one for spiritual and the other for temporal affairs. But both curates were animated by the same moral purpose, and that is the sufficient and effective unity. *The state must be self-contained.* This principle follows from the previous one, for if a state is dependent on an external state for any of its necessities, to that extent the authority within the state will be diminished. Its influence will leak out in bales of goods and bills of exchange, and a competing authority, all the more dangerous for being invisible and impalpable, will become established. *The state must be armed against invasion.* Again a dependent principle, for an unarmed state will provoke the envy of predatory neighbours. *The state must be incorruptible,* or, as we might say, armed against sedition. Sedition is only provoked by injustice, but injustice implies not only the failure to administer the laws established for the common good, but also the existence of unimpeachable injustices, chief of which is the inequality of wealth.

The more I studied their history, the more firmly I became convinced that the Jesuits had only failed for one reason: they had provoked the envy of princes and marauders, first by their accumulation of wealth, and then by their inability to defend themselves against invasion.

I had no difficulty in securing the consent of the Council to certain measures designed to enforce these principles of government. My own salary, and the pay of all officers and officials, was fixed at low but adequate figures, sufficient to support a decent household, but not enough to leave an unused surplus. The professional army, except for a cadre of officers, was abolished, but each family was required to supply one able-bodied male, who should be liable to remain under arms until a relief was provided. To secure the homogeneity of the state, marriage between Spaniards was forbidden—the assimilation of all foreign elements was thereby automatically secured. No foreigner was to be allowed entry into the state except under licence; he could only settle in the state by taking a native wife. All inequalities of status were abolished—every human being had equal rights in law. The freehold of all land was assumed by the state, and all landowners or estancerias were required to conduct their estates for the common benefit, on pain of forfeiture. The only distinction remaining would arise from the division of labour: one man must govern a farm, as one authority a state; but inasmuch as the capabilities of men vary, so their functions should vary; yet not their rewards.

Though the laws securing these principles were enacted in the first year of our government, it naturally took many years for all the necessary adjustments to be made. Certain rebel elements, Spaniards all, had to be deported. Certain merchants declared themselves bankrupt; they were offered estates in the prairie-lands, or given the alternative of leaving the country. Certain estancerias resented the impounding of their surplus produce, but again the only alternative offered to them was emigration. In general, the difficulties were not such as would be anticipated in an older civilisation. Though slavery had not been unknown in Roncador, and though the lowest grades of peasants were ignorant and impoverished, there existed no social barriers. It was, the Spaniards apart, a classless society, and our only problem was to devise means of equalising the wealth of all the members of this society.

Briefly, our method, introduced gradually, was to set apart a certain number of days' labour for the benefit of the individual labourer, another portion for the benefit of the state. That portion set aside for the state was supervised by the estanceria, who collected the produce and from it took enough for his own needs. The surplus for the state was collected in barns and warehouses in each town and district, and there exchanged against the produce of the mechanical arts. Thus a shoemaker in the town would exchange, at a fixed rate, a pair of shoes for so much tea, tobacco, beef, or corn. The surplus of this local barter was collected in the capital, and there bartered with merchants against imports of foreign manufacture. Such imports were of various classes— those for distribution, such as salt and articles of adornment; and those for the direct use of the state, such as equipment for the army. The excess of exports over imports might accumulate as a reserve of credit in the accounts of the foreign importers; an excess of imports was not under any circumstances permitted.

Such was our simple economy, and I do not flatter myself by imagining that its design is one to be imitated in more complicated civilisations. But its suitability to the State of Roncador was never in doubt; at the end of the first three years of government there was a general air of peace and contentment. Men and women lived in a relationship of mutual confidence, cultivating the earth and living happily on the abundance of its fruits.

One unforeseen result followed. At the end of three years it was necessary, under the terms of the Constitution, to summon a General Assembly and re-elect a Council of Government. As the time for this event came near, I visited in turn each of the three Governors. I first went to Hermanegildo Chora. He had continually excused himself from attending meetings of the Council on the grounds of his age and infirmity. I found him seated on his verandah, his silvery white hair shining against the darkened interior. He had reached the age of eighty-three and begged that he might now be left in peace. He was confident that the conduct of affairs was in competent hands, and for his part he was content to leave the government of the state to its executive officers.

I then went to see Don Pasqual Arapatî. I found him busy watching over the gathering of the yerba plants—an operation requiring skill in one of its processes, when the leaves are scorched over an open fire before being stripped from the branches. He kept me out in the open fields until the end of the day's labour, and then insisted on my company at dinner, which was held in the estancia, master and men all sitting together at one table and eating from the same dishes. It was a scene of great animation, overpowering in its gusto and its sweaty repletion. It was not until we had reached the final stage of cigars that I found an opportunity of explaining my mission. Don Pasqual would scarcely listen to me. 'When you return,' he said, 'tell the Assembly that they have the best government in the world, and that only fools will interfere with it.' For himself, he added, he was too busy to meddle further in the affairs of the state. It was work for learned men, such as Don Hermanegildo and General Santos.

You will see, therefore, that by the time I reached the farm of General Santos I was not a little perplexed. I found my friend as I always remembered him, with humming-birds fluttering round his quills of syrup, in odd community with these tamed creatures. When I had told him of the attitude of his two fellow-councillors towards the question of re-election, he smiled philosophically, and seemed in no way disturbed. He promised, however, to consider the matter, and to come to the Assembly with new proposals.

I therefore summoned the caciques on the appointed day. But first one and then another messenger came back, with a request that the cacique should be excused from attending the General Assembly: there was much to be done on his estate and he could not afford to leave it for the several days required for a visit to the capital. Altogether more than two hundred caciques sent messages to this effect, many adding that they were content to be governed by Don Olivero and his Council.

I naturally sent alarmed messages to General Santos, but he made no comments. The day of the election arrived, but there was no more stir in Roncador than on an ordinary market day. Perhaps eighty caciques came with their families, but not all of these deigned to attend the meeting in the cathedral. At the appointed hour General Santos and I entered from the cloister, accompanied by Iturbide. I spoke to the small gathering and explained the necessity, under the terms of the Constitution, of now electing a new Council, to replace the Council which had served its legal term of three years. Don Hermanegildo Chora and Don Pasqual Arapatî, I announced, felt constrained to retire from their onerous duties, the one on account of his great age, the other because he wished to devote himself entirely to the cultivation of his estate. It was therefore the duty of the Assembly to propose two new members for the honour of serving on the Council.

General Santos then spoke to the Assembly. He too, he said, would like to retire from active participation in the government of the country. He had served Roncador all his life, and now wished to devote his last years to the pleasures of a country life. He had come to the

Assembly for the last time, not to accept re-election, not to propose a successor, but merely to transfer the authority of the existing Council to the Council to be elected.

I then called for the names of the new candidates for election, but there was no response. Here and there groups of caciques began to talk animatedly to each other, without, however, making any proposals to the meeting. We waited for ten minutes or so, and then after a consultation with General Santos, we decided to adjourn the meeting for one hour to enable the delegates to come to some decision. I made an announcement accordingly, and then retired with the General and Iturbide to the barracks. There we had a consultation among ourselves, and decided that if no nominations were forthcoming, a proposal should be made to continue a provisional government under my direction, with the existing Council as a consultative committee.

We duly returned to the Assembly, and found it very much dispersed; many delegates had departed for their dinners, and the rest were arguing in groups, but judging from the few words I overheard, mainly on matters of cattle and crops, they were not exercised about the affairs of government. Called to silence, and asked for their decision, a tall and commanding creole stepped forward. 'Gentlemen,' he said, 'why should we waste our time here? We are well governed by Don Olivero; he is learned in the art of government; let him therefore continue to rule us without hindrance. When we are dissatisfied, we can meet here again.' This proposal was received with acclamation, and the Assembly broke up without leaving me time to protest, or to make even a pretence of modesty.

In this manner I became sole governor of the state of

Roncador, a position I was to occupy for twenty-five years. When I look back I find it very difficult to convey even to myself any sense of the sequence of events which filled such a long stretch of time. Most of my early difficulties were practical ones, but in the two spheres where most trouble was to be anticipated, the Church and the Army, I was aided by subordinates who had no ambitions of their own, and who were pleased to exercise obediently and with understanding the authority I delegated to them. Iturbide was made General and Commander-in-Chief of the military forces. He administered the system of compulsory service with tact and efficiency, and on the rare occasions on which the forces were called into action to deal with raiders or threats of invasion, he displayed a cunning and bravery which in the battlefields of Europe would have earned him immortal renown. But events in Roncador were not normally reported to the outside world, so Iturbide had to be satisfied with the gratitude of his Governor and the love of his people.

The Church proved a far more difficult problem, but the Paî Lorenzo had continued to win my confidence and respect, so that when at last the old and feeble-minded Bishop died, I insisted on the translation of this worthy father. I told him that the Church would be allowed full liberty and authority in all spiritual matters, so long as it conducted itself according to the principles of its Founder, teaching men to love each other, adopting for its priesthood a rule of poverty and chastity, attending to the sick and the dying, and performing all other corporal acts of mercy. Bishop Lorenzo had no other wish, but the task of cleansing the priesthood was one of great difficulty. To have unfrocked all that were corrupt would have left half the parishes in Roncador without a curate. A seminary was established for the training of new priests, and as soon as new priests were fit and ordained they took the place of the corrupted. In a very few years the example made of the worst offenders had a very sobering effect on the rest, but it was a long time before the process of purification was complete.

The art of government is the art of delegating authority. It is essential that the authority delegated should be held like a ball on an elastic string: it does not matter how large the ball, or how far the string is stretched, provided authority returns to its source at the inflection of a finger. The ideal governor is one who has dispossessed himself of *all* authority, remaining merely as the mathematical centre in whom a thousand lines converge: the invisible, perhaps only the potential, manipulator of a host of efficient marionettes. In more complex states the system of delegation will be divided and subdivided, but such was the simplicity of the economy of Roncador that I myself was able to control directly every post of administration.

When finally the machine of government was working without friction of any kind, I began to employ my energies in the supervision of communal improvements. The funds in our treasury grew year by year, but I was determined to expend them as quickly as they accumulated, for idle money is money wasted. I therefore devised plans for the improvement of the capital, and of the communications leading to it. Arming myself with theodolite and chains, I surveyed the streets and surrounding spaces, decreed orientations and elevations, ordered demolitions and rebuilding. I had the quarry from which the Jesuits extracted granite for their buildings reopened, and with this stone repaved the principal streets of Roncador, built a hospital for the sick, and gradually replaced the miserable huts in which most of the inhabitants lived by structures of a more solid nature. At first some of these works were looked upon with disapproval, especially as they involved the compulsory use of private vehicles and the organisation of free service. But once the improvements began to assume a visible reality the citizens of Roncador took pride and pleasure in the enterprise, and yearly the city increased its beauty and practical convenience.

I lavished a good deal of the state's income on the improvement of the army. The latest rifles were imported, and all our military equipment was of the fashions prevalent in Europe. I myself designed a new uniform, brighter and more elegant than any known in South America. My principle here was to give the greatest grandeur to the lower ranks. Except for certain details, the army was entirely a corps of mounted rifles. The privates wore a scarlet tunic, with a plastron and girdle of gold braid, and peach-yellow trousers of cuirassier cut. The collars and cuffs of the tunics were peach-yellow, with dove-grey piping; the shoulder-straps dove-grey with yellow piping. Boots and head-dress were of black hide, the latter adorned on the left side with a silver cockade. The officers, whose numbers and ranks had been drastically reduced, wore uniforms which were of severe cut, devoid of facings, differing between each rank only in the colour of the tunics. The Commander-in-Chief wore the uniform trousers, with a tunic of black, epaulettes and cockade of gold.

For myself, I took care to avoid any form of ostentation. I was seen invariably in a cloak, knee-breeches, and sombrero, all of black. In Roncador I lived simply in two rooms on the first floor of the barracks; I was attended by one personal servant. Nevertheless I recognised that a people is not happy without ritual, and that a government must avoid at all costs an effect of drabness and dull passivity. I therefore had guards mounted daily with ceremony in front of the Government House (as the barracks were now called), and on all festivals and holidays the whole army appeared in the splendour of parade order. On these occasions I appeared in public, mounted on a white horse, and received the full ceremonial salute of the assembled troops. Usually, however, I maintained an impenetrable reserve. I relaxed before none of my subordinates, and was never seen indulging in any popular pleasures. My only recreations were those I shared with General Santos, and after his death with his son, who succeeded to his estate. There I would often resort for the pleasures of the country, for shooting and bathing, and there eventually I built a small lodge, where I might keep a few possessions—my rifles, my fishing-rods, and a small library of books.

So the years passed, undisturbed by war or rebellion. In all this time only one incident of a violent nature ever took place, and this was partly of my own seeking. It occurred in the fourth year of my dictatorship, and in this manner:

In the great pampas to the south and east of Roncador, vast tracts of country beyond the control of the governments to which they nominally belonged, there arose from time to time bands of freebooters who existed by raiding on land and by piracy on the river. They were the terror of all the native settlements, and interfered seriously with the establishment of commercial relations between the interior and Buenos Ayres. The political uncertainty of the situation gave them every encouragement, especially in the form of recruits, experienced in arms and desperate in deeds. Among these marauders a leader had arisen, Vargas by name, to which he added the indispensable title of General. He gathered under his command about a thousand followers, mainly Indians, and all admirable horsemen. Their chief needs —pasture for their horses and cattle to slaughter for food—were satisfied without much danger or difficulty on the wide and fertile plains on which they made their home. But for other essentials, of which the most important was ammunition, and for luxuries like wine and clothing, they were dependent on the river traffic.

At the time of which I speak, General Vargas had established a camp about a hundred miles to the south of the rapids which marked the boundary of Roncador. It was a well-chosen spot, for the river there opened out into a wide and sluggish reach, in the middle of which stretched a low but luxuriantly wooded island. Vargas would hold up a vessel from the shore, which thus engaged would then be taken by surprise by a boatful of ruffians advancing swiftly from under the cover of the island.

At first he made no attempt to interfere with vessels bound for Roncador, but eventually, made bold by the general immunity he seemed to enjoy, he rifled a cargo of arms and uniforms, and held the trader in charge of it a prisoner in the camp. This insolence was not to be tolerated, and knowing that any protests to the government nominally responsible for Vargas would be useless, I determined to act in the interests of the general security of the country. I decided, moreover, to lead this punitive expedition myself. For although I enjoyed the respect of all the citizens as an administrator, I had never taken part in any military action, and my pride suffered a little from the suspicion that my courage might be doubted. Experience had already led me to the conclusion that though the distinction between men of action and men of imagination is a fundamental one, it by no means follows that courage is the exclusive possession of the former class. Indeed, I was rather of the opinion, which further experience was to confirm, that the physically forceful type of man is often at heart a coward, ready to crumble up in situations of extreme danger; whilst the feebler introspective type, by virtue of the transforming power of his imagination, is much more capable of decisive action. Courage is the ability to act as if death were a fantasy.

I elaborated the plans for our expedition with the help of Iturbide. Surprise was to be the determining factor, for I had no desire to engage our whole army in the affair. We decided to attack Vargas's camp from the river and from land, simultaneously, and judged that a force of about 150 men would be sufficient. Iturbide with a company of a hundred mounted men was to proceed overland to an agreed point, where he would await a signal from the river party. For the river our plans were more elaborate. They consisted in fitting out two vessels of the kind known as piraguas, which were much in use for heavy transport on the river. In shape these vessels were like a huge box, square and flat at the bottom, with sloping sides which met a square deck of about twice the area of the bottom. Round the rim of this decapitated and inverted pyramid a gallery or gangway was built, sufficiently broad to allow rowers to stand conveniently upon it. The piragua was usually loaded with bales, square with the top of it, and on the top of the bales a deck of loose boards was laid, on which other cargo could be loaded, leaving a space for a cabin roofed with hides. Such a vessel, capable of carrying a load of 200 tons, is floated down the river, steered as well as may be by means of the oars.

We constructed two of these vessels, but instead of bales of yerba and hides we put on bales of sand of about the same size and appearance, but leaving a hollow space within the middle of the vessel, and loopholes between the bales. We built, in fact, two floating fort-resses, each garrisoned by twenty-four rifles.

The piragua travels slowly, at not more than four miles an hour. I calculated, therefore, that it would take us almost exactly twenty-four hours to reach a point near Vargas's camp. We decided to attack soon after dawn, when most of Vargas's followers would still be sunk in the heavy sleep which followed their nightly debauch.

We waited for a full moon, to enable us to negotiate the river by night, and early one morning I departed with the two piraguas. Iturbide was to follow later with the horsemen, who would travel more quickly to the agreed point. I placed myself on the top of one of the great tubs, and all that day we travelled pleasantly enough, our main difficulty being to keep the two vessels within reasonable distance of each other, for every now and then one of us would get taken up in an eddy, which kept us spinning on our own axis for a considerable time.

The night was still and clear, the sky brilliant. The wooded banks were silent, and our clumsy and log-like motion seemed an intrusion on the placid elements around us. The men took turns at steering and sleeping, but I was far too excited by the event, and far too exalted by the beauty of the night, to do aught but stare ahead. The point where we were to concert with Iturbide was marked by a bend in the river, and a sandy beach, not easy to miss. We reached it about an hour before dawn, and steered our vessels against the opposite bank, where we fastened them to the trunks of stout trees.

The forest behind us began to stir with life; a choir of birds filled the air with liquid or piercing notes; monkeys began to chatter in the overhanging branches. The light came suddenly and hushed this overture, and then I saw a rider come down to the opposite beach and give the signal: a white handkerchief waved three times in a semicircle. This meant that all was well with Iturbide, and that the attack could proceed. I gave the agreed response, and ordered the vessels to unmoor, and the unoccupied men to stand to their arms. It was still about three miles to the camp, but our progress was unhindered, and in half an hour we were at the opening of the broad reach, with the island in front of us. As soon as we were well within the current that ran to the left of the island, and therefore nearest the camp, I had a rope thrown between the vessels, to keep them together, and except for four men with oars to act as rudder, all were alert at their loopholes.

We were now within four hundred yards of the landing-stage, and it was necessary, in accordance with our plan, to create an immediate diversion. But there was not a human being in sight, and the actual tents and huts of Vargas's camp were in dead ground. I had no alternative, therefore, but to send a volley aimlessly shorewards. It had its effect, however, for a stray bullet wounded a tethered horse, which began to scream in its pain. Two or three figures now appeared, and gazed in the direction of our shots. I now ordered three men with rifles to appear on deck, and then to kneel and take aim, as if they constituted our firing party. We drifted closer, and then took a single shot at the figures on the shore. They retired, and angry shouts were heard in the distance. We had drifted perhaps a hundred yards nearer when a considerable body of men appeared with rifles and cried out across the river, presumably threatening us or calling on us to pull in to shore. I ordered everyone on board to take shelter behind the sandbags, and opened fire again on the shore. We were now so close, and they so dense, that several men were hit and fell. The rest retreated to the edge of the beach, where there was a ridge of high grass and bushes, and from this vantage-point they opened fire on the vessels, which, deprived of their steering oars, drifted somewhat aimlessly in the slow current. But here the advantage of the piragua became evident, for whichever way we swerved we presented a broadside towards the shore. We now kept up a continuous fire, which was answered by an increasing volume from the river bank; but their bullets for the most part buried themselves harmlessly in the sandbags, or went astray. Only occasionally a chance shot penetrated a loophole, and in this manner two of the men in my piragua were wounded, and another, in the second vessel, killed.

We were now so near the critical moment that I was sick with suspense and excitement. The current had carried us midstream, which was as I had hoped; for by the time we were opposite the small landing-stage which Vargas had built, our rifles were getting hot, and the acrid stench of powder almost stifled us in our confined space; to have drifted into the shallows near the shore would have delayed our progress and prolonged the fighting. But this was the concerted moment for Iturbide to ride down on the camp from the opposite direction. It was impossible to hear anything above the sound of our own firing, but the sudden cessation of firing from the shore was the only indication we needed. I rushed up to the deck, and at first could see nothing; but the hubbub told me that Iturbide was there with his men.

Presently, away to the south, I saw a scattered troop of men riding like furies across a bare slope, obviously in flight.

The rowers had now resumed their positions, and directed the vessels towards the bank, which we reached about half a mile below the landing-stage. I sent a man on shore to find a vantage-point and report the situation. He returned almost immediately, accompanied by a scout on horseback, sent to meet us by Iturbide. Our plan had been more successful than we had believed possible. Iturbide and his troops had swept on the camp unperceived. Already alarmed by the attack from the river, the whole camp was in a state of confusion. Here and there a desperate man had fired from behind a hut or a tent. Many had dashed half clothed to the horse ranks and ridden away without stopping to harness. The rest were being disarmed and driven on to the beach.

Taking the scout's horse, I galloped towards the camp. Our plan would not be completely successful unless Vargas himself was taken, dead or alive. Desultory firing was still to be heard, coming from the direction of the camp. I kept to the river bank and in a few minutes came upon some of our own men, guarding a crowd of about two hundred prisoners, who had been driven like sheep on to the crescent-shaped beach. Iturbide was with the party still clearing up the camp, so I hastened off in that direction.

The camp was a straggling assemblage of hovels, mostly constructed of hides. In the centre a space was cleared round a wooden hut of a more substantial kind, which was Vargas's headquarters. Here a party still kept up resistance, firing from windows and loopholes. A shot greeted me as I came within range, grazing my right shoulder. I hastily dismounted, and then approached gradually, availing myself of the plentiful cover afforded by the hovels. In this manner I reached the position from which Iturbide with about twenty men was covering the hut. Iturbide himself was there, but it was no occasion for greetings. I indicated that he was to retain charge of the situation, and myself took up a firing position behind a heap of hides.

The party in the hut could not number more than six or seven men, and their position was quite a hopeless one. Iturbide had given instructions to his men to cover the hut, but only to fire in answer to shots from the hut. After two hours of this slow duel, and after a silence of half an hour, we decided to rush the hut and batter in the door with a tree trunk. But whilst we were preparing this manœuvre the door of the hut was suddenly flung open, and an unarmed man came towards us. He walked slowly and deliberately, and when within speaking distance of us, lifted up his hand with a gesture of resignation and cried: 'It is all over. The General is dying.' There was no reason to doubt such a dispirited hostage. We went forward and found the mud floor of the hut strewn with the bodies of wounded and dead men. An additional grimness was lent to the scene by the bullocks' skulls against which some of the wounded were leaning. These objects were often used as stools in a camp of this kind, but now, embraced by these desperate men, they seemed like symbols of death.

Vargas was shot through the throat, and died speechless. There were altogether about forty dead, including seven of our own men. We laid their bodies against the wooden hut and built a vast pyre of the camp material, and then set fire to it all. The stores of ammunition were taken to the beach, to await a vessel proceeding to Roncador. There still remained the prisoners to dispose of;

the actual number of them was an embarrassment. We had no desire to keep them as prisoners, nor even to punish them for the misdemeanours of Vargas. We decided to load them on the piraguas and set them drifting down the river without oars. This involved a certain amount of reconstruction of the vessels, and it was nearly nightfall before we had accomplished everything. We then took a number of captured horses and rode away into the night. The funeral pyre still burned with a lurid light in the darkness behind us; before us the stars hung above Roncador. In spite of our victory, we were silent; only the creaking of our saddles, and the jingle of our equipment, rose above the soft thunder of hooves.

I had played a comparatively inactive part in the attack; the greatest danger had fallen to Iturbide, and on Iturbide I laid the formal honours of rank and reward. But a people, once it has made an individual the apex of its authority, is anxious to gild him like an idol with all the virtues in its code. By this one brief and insignificant episode I became for the citizens of Roncador the embodiment of their national glory.

My public works, extending over many years and costing me much thought and anxiety, had no such epic value. They were the tyrannical and absolute aspect of my dictatorship, and were accepted with appreciation or respect, but never with jubilation. They depended entirely for their accomplishment on the singular energy of my own mind, which drove me restlessly from one task to another. When I was reasonably satisfied with the plan of the capital, with its public buildings and its streets; when the army had been reformed and refitted—then I turned to smaller improvements: to the laying out of public gardens, to the design of tokens of exchange and currency-notes and to devising a national flag: a black

phœnix rising against a yellow ground, with a red ball
for the sun above its head. But soon even these tasks
came to an end, and I was forced more and more to
employ myself with my own thoughts, to conduct a
philosophical examination of all I had achieved, to
weigh the present against the future.

I perceived that my course had led me far away from
the guiding principles of the revolutionary writers who
had been my first inspiration. I could feel satisfied that I
had adhered to the fundamental ideas on which any
humane society must be based—the central dogmas of
equality, fraternity and justice. But these ideas are vague
enough to admit of very diverse interpretations. In de-
creeing the isolation of Roncador from the other free
republics of America I had ensured the success of our
experiment; but I had affirmed our indifference to the
lot of the rest of the world, and our fraternal spirit, for
example, had not extended beyond our boundaries. This
had led to an early breach with the Society of Patriots
in Buenos Ayres—a breach I deeply regretted. I was not
prepared, however, to sacrifice the tangible freedom of
our own republic for the doubtful fruits of a grand
alliance with others less firmly established. I feared that
our liberty of action might be compromised by international commitments.

The whole course of my dictatorship was marked by
a complete indifference to what my pattern, Napoleon
Buonaparte, had called *ideological* projects; by the complete absence, that is to say, of any desire to uplift the
state to the level of visionary speculations. If we had
created an Utopia, it was a worldly and actual Utopia,
made out of existing materials. I did not step beyond
the aspirations of the simple peasantry which was the
bulk of our population. I could not regard any other

function in the state as more honourable or more desirable than the cultivation of the earth; and since this is an occupation which employs all the energy and faculties of a normal man, it would have been a treason to the state to educate men above that station. Even the simple elements of reading and writing did not seem to be of much moment in our policy; for what little clerical work was necessary in a community could be done by the priests, who were excellently trained in the seminary established at Roncador.

I acted from day to day, always on the principle of removing any causes of friction, of making equality and fraternity realities, and justice the normal procedure. Against such a policy there is no possibility of revolt; for any immoral and anti-social tendencies will be individual and self-proclaimed, powerless against the general will for good.

Such being the stability and happiness of our state, it may seem incredible that doubts should have entered my mind. At first the doubts were not formulated as such; I was merely seized by an uncontrollable depression, which I vainly tried to trace to climatic or physical conditions. But it soon became clear to me that the causes were mental, that I was enveloped in a spiritual lassitude for which profounder explanations were necessary. No form of activity, neither my hunting-lodge nor my library, could assuage my restless and dissatisfied mind.

This condition lasted for several years, until finally I could no longer evade the truth. My spiritual complaint was produced by the very stagnation around me which I regarded as the triumph of my policy. In the absence of conflict, of contending interests, of anguish and agitation, I had induced into my environment a moral flaccidity, a fatness of living, an ease and a torpor which had now produced in me an inevitable ferment. I knew that such a mental disease had afflicted the monasteries in the Middle Ages, when they attempted to draw away from the world of action and live a life of contemplation. It is true that mine was not a life of contemplation, but it was becoming one of intellectual abstraction. So long as the republic was unformed, I was occupied in practical affairs. My ideas were immediately translated into action. But now no action was called for; my mind felt no resistance in facts, no tension in circumstance.

In my speculations at this time I began to suspect that the Golden Age, of which such strong traditions exist in many parts of the world, may indeed have existed, but that it decayed for the very reasons which were now becoming apparent to me. Without eccentric elements, no progress is possible; not even that simple progress which consists in whipping a spinning top from one place to another.

Try as I would, I could not solve my personal problem in social terms. I might have introduced a system of education, and thus have created a society of intellectual beings. I might in that way have put an end to my boredom, but I should have disrupted the peace of the state by creating a class absorbed in visionary speculations, eager to translate their ideological projects into action. As I watched the Indians peacefully going about their work in the estancias, or the inhabitants of Roncador walking in the gardens, sitting in the shade by the fountains, everywhere mirthful and contented, I dismissed such ideas. Better that I myself should perish than that their serenity should be shattered.

Along with this spiritual development, another change took place in my mental life which was to influence the decision I eventually made. I found my thoughts more and more reverting to the period of my childhood and youth. Again, my lack of an active occupation may have been the cause; and perhaps in any case we all become more reminiscent as we grow older, especially if we are exiles in a foreign land. But year by year these recollections grew more vivid, rose up from depths I had never realised, crowded in upon my daily thoughts. I developed an extreme longing or nostalgia for my native country. I lived over again all my childish experiences, my days at school and college, my humiliation as a schoolmaster. But vivid as all these actual recollections were, I was most haunted by the thought of an experience missed—the appearance in my village of the green children. I longed to know how that mystery had been solved, what had become of them in the course of the years. I began to create an ideal image of them as they had grown up in our alien world: beings half-human and half-angel, intermediate between the grossness of earth and the purity of heaven.

I resolved to escape. But I could not simply take leave of a country that had been so long identified with my life, the creation of my mind. Let alone the sentimental difficulties of such a step, any such deliberate action on my part would have a debilitating effect on the morale of the country. I should have to nominate a successor, and to reinitiate all the obsolete machinery of popular assembly and election. In my state of mind, such proceedings would have been an impossibility. I must therefore disappear suddenly, but without the effect of desertion. My leaving must have the contrary effect of moral and political stimulus. I must depart in a cloud of glory.

At length I conceived that the only method which would give all the desirable results would be that of assassination; but since I desired to survive and escape to England, it must be a mock assassination.

So much decided, certain principles then determined the elaboration of my plans. The motive for assassination must be one that would bind the people together more firmly than ever. It must not be attributable to any dissatisfaction or revolt within the state. It must therefore be the work of an alien; it must represent an attempt on the integrity and independence of Roncador itself.

I elaborated my plans slowly, with infinite precaution. It was some time before the heaven-sent opportunity occurred, but I felt the promise of solution one day when I received a visit from a North American prospector. He asked my permission to make a survey of the mountains on the eastern boundaries of Roncador. An old tradition of the Indians spoke of former gold-mines in this region, though no gold had been discovered there by the Spaniards.

In ordinary circumstances I should have dismissed this adventurer at once, for the exploitation of such a commodity would completely upset the balanced economy of the state, lead to the external envy which had ruined the establishments of the Jesuits, and generally introduce a commercial spirit into our midst which would be disruptive of our harmony and modest contentment. But I stifled my reaction to the proposal, and gave the man permission to make a preliminary survey, on condition that he acted with discretion and that his reports were delivered direct to me, and that no further action in the matter should be taken without my consent.

In about two months' time the prospector returned. His survey had been successful beyond any expectations. Not only did rich veins exist in the hills, but the river which ran parallel to them for so great a distance was rich in deposits of ore. This suited my plan. I told the prospector that I would now consider his application for a concession to mine the gold, and meanwhile asked him to take up his residence in Roncador.

There I kept him waiting for several weeks, without giving a decision. He was a man of unscrupulous character, and before long I was informed by spies that he had begun a correspondence with his principals in Buenos Ayres, and that a plot of the usual kind was hatching. A neighbouring state was to be enlisted by the financial corruption of its government, induced to pick a quarrel with Roncador, and then to invade us with all the forces which the prospect of gold can command.

I now took Iturbide into my confidence. I did not reveal to him my final aim, which he would, in his simplicity, have found incomprehensible. But I showed him the prospector's report, and gave him full details of the intrigue that was hatching. I confessed to a stupidity in ever allowing the prospector to enter Roncador, and asked his aid in countering the plot.

To dismiss the prospector, I explained, was out of the question. That would merely facilitate his plans. To imprison him, or execute him on a vague charge of conspiracy, would involve us in a quarrel with a powerful nation. We must wait and watch until we had sufficient evidence to convince the world that we had acted in accordance with the precepts of international justice, and in self-defence. Iturbide promised to keep a strict watch on all movements on the frontier, and to be ready to act swiftly in an emergency.

I then completed the personal part of my plans. I wrote a political testament, very simple and short, setting forth the principles on which I had governed Roncador for more than twenty years. I indicated that I had done this as a general precaution, in the spirit of a wise father who provides for his children; and I recommended Iturbide to the country as my successor. This document I deposited with the Clerk of the Archives, with instructions that it was only to be opened in the event of my death.

I then, in the privacy of my hunting-lodge, made a blasting charge of considerable power. I had, of course, a free supply of powder for my shooting cartridges, and the military handbooks in my possession gave detailed instructions for the blowing up of bridges, railways and fortifications.

I have already described the bridge of three arches which crossed the river on the west of Roncador. This bridge I crossed whenever I went to my country retreat, and here in prospect I staged my mock assassination. In the course of my building activities I had at one time made a thorough examination of the structure, and had then decided to leave it standing, for the Jesuits who had built it had built well. Though supported by two piers, the bridge was a single arch ring springing from the rocky banks of the river; the points of highest pressure were therefore situated at the crown and springings, and a charge, to be effective, must be placed within the stress of the arch, and not in the piers. I decided that the most effective point of all would be near the actual crown.

The road-bed of the bridge was constructed of granite sets, about nine inches square, and was slightly cambered. Centuries of use had worn ruts at each side, and the intermediate blocks had become loosened in some cases. Returning from my lodge early one morning, I sent my servant on ahead with the horses, and, lingering on the bridge, perceived that it would be a simple matter to lift one of the blocks near the crown. I reckoned that if I placed the charge under one of these blocks, firmly wedging it in, I should have sufficient tamping to make the explosion effective. The whole operation could be completed in five or ten minutes.

When my materials, which included ten feet of fuse, were ready, I waited for a favourable occasion. I required two conditions: a river in spate and a moonlit night. I counted also on finding a canoe beached on the river bank, at a point just below the bridge where the Indians had a primitive landing-stage.

Finally, towards the middle of July, such conditions were promised, and I determined to act. I announced my intention of spending a week at my hunting-lodge, and asked Iturbide to deal with any minor affairs that arose during my absence. I then departed, accompanied by my servant alone.

The second night of my absence, I waited until two o'clock in the morning, and then awoke my servant, showing him a letter I had myself prepared. I told him that I had been summoned to Roncador and must depart at once. Ordering him to saddle my horse, I packed my materials and was ready as soon as the horse. I told my servant to wait until dawn, and then follow me with my usual baggage. I then rode away, the path clear before me in the moonlight.

When I arrived within a hundred yards of the bridge, I left my horse untethered, and approached the bridge on foot. The moon was high in the sky above me; in front of me I could see the outlines of Roncador, huddled and silent on the hill, the white walls of a few buildings glimmering out of the darker mass. I looked over the parapet and saw the long black outlines of three canoes on the bank below. The river ran swiftly, its currents coiling together in the oily glaze of the moonlight.

I had brought with me a cold chisel, and had no difficulty in dislodging one of the granite blocks. The masonry below was broken and loose, so that without difficulty I scratched a hollow in the fabric of the arch. There I placed my charge of gunpowder, with the fuse ready fixed. I tamped it in with paper I had brought, and then with the dislodged rubble, finally replacing the granite block which I firmly prised against its neighbours with wooden wedges.

I worked rapidly and in ten minutes all was ready. My horse had wandered down towards the bridge, but I must move him out of danger. I led him back along the road a hundred yards or so, and there said good-bye to an animal that was more dear to me than any human being. He did not comprehend my actions, but stayed where I bid him stay; his presence there, riderless after the explosion, was an essential detail of my plot.

I returned to the bridge and took a final look round. As a last precaution I went down to the bank and drew one of the canoes down to the water's edge. There was nothing else to detain me. I hastened back to the crown of the bridge, and under the shelter of the parados lit the fuse. I watched it splutter for an inch or two, and then ran back to the canoe. I pushed out into the current and floated away on its flood.

It seemed an age before a loud detonation rent the air. I was far away by then, but presently I saw a cloud of dusty smoke drift across the face of the moon, and still later my boat rocked in the swell caused by the explosion.

3

THE water had no sooner closed over them than it seemed to be sucked away from their bodies, to curve upwards at their feet, to arch over their heads, until it formed a perfect spheroid. They were standing within an immense bubble, against which the water pressed in vain, the sandy particles quivering rapidly against its glassy inner wall. At first they were aware of a motion of descent, but soon this ceased, and they would not have known that they were moving but for the agitation of the water outside their bubble.

Olivero still held the hand of the Green Child, but they did not look at each other; they felt indifferently. Time and its anguish were abolished; they felt a little sleepy.

Then the water broke above their heads and without having experienced any sense of reversal they ascended in the middle of a pool. They found themselves in a large grotto, filled with an aqueous light, blue in the darker reaches, pale green towards the apparent outlet. A rocky basin, rising in many green and mossy ledges, filled the floor of the grotto. The walls were irregular, and from the roof hung long glassy icicles, sometimes so long that they touched the floor and made round columns, tapering inwards towards their axes.

Full self-awareness returned to them as soon as they were free of the water; they instantly struggled towards the rocky shore, which they reached without difficulty. The air about them was extremely warm, about equal to that of a glasshouse in summer; so that they did not feel incommoded by their clothes, which had become wet as they waded to the shore. But whether from the closeness of the air, or the mental agitation of the experience he had just passed through, Olivero began to feel faint, and sank to the ground. There he rested until he became accustomed to the atmosphere, the Green Child sitting by his side. When he had recovered, she told him that this was surely her native country, from which she and her brother had strayed thirty years ago.

When they had rested there about an hour, they got up and made for that end of the grotto which seemed to admit light. The grotto gradually contracted, and the entrance, when they reached it, was not above four feet high. They proceeded in a crouching attitude and soon came out, but not into what we should call the open; for though the space that they now gazed into was much larger than that of the grotto they had left, nevertheless a roof arched wide over them, higher and of greater span than the interior of any cathedral. The light in this space was still dim, like the summer twilight in England, but of a distinct greenish tinge. Olivero now perceived that it was emitted from the walls of the vast cavern, and must be of a phosphorescent nature. The rock itself was of a crystalline formation.

Another phenomenon that immediately struck him was a sound of faint bells, which seemed to come from every direction. When he turned to the Green Child for an explanation, she pointed to an overhanging ledge, from which hung, suspended on strings, a series of rods varying in length from eighteen inches to about three feet. Agitated in the gentle breezes which circulated round the cavern, the rods struck against each other and gave off the bell-like tones which Olivero heard. Later he discovered that these rods were of innumerable dimensions, the smallest being prismatic needles of crystalline rock two or three inches long, which tinkled like a child's musical box, the largest being long rods of rock as much as twenty feet long, which emitted notes as deep and sombre as any metal bell. These larger rods were in fact stalagmites whose formation had been controlled over a long period of time, to ensure regularity of mass and consequent purity of tone. Special caverns, which might be regarded as workshops or factories, were set apart for this purpose.

The Green Child told Olivero that these bells or gongs were hung everywhere about the country to guide people from one part to another; for each direction had its particular note or chime and only by listening for this sound could an inhabitant of a country without sun or stars tell which way to go. All notes, or chimes, could be traced back to the centre of this underground world; but if ever anyone strayed out of range of the bells, into uninhabited caverns or grottoes, they would lose all sense of direction, and might never find their way back again. It was in this manner that she had strayed into the cavern whose pool sank to the outer world.

Listening now to the bells, they followed where the sound led, which was from one cavern to another, some of which were wide and immensely high, others long and narrow like a tunnel, others like a honeycomb of fissures. The same luminescence pervaded them all. The majority were dry—at least the majority of those they walked through; but in others water dripped from the roofs or ran down the walls to the rock bed, where it collected in pools. Here and there clear streams ran along channels cut in the floor, very narrow and in some cases obviously chiselled out by hand. The water was slightly cooler than the air, and though somewhat sulphurous, pleasant to drink.

The only kind of growth that could be compared to

vegetation were various kinds of fungus-like plants growing from the walls of the caves. In the larger grottoes
these were often of a coral-like structure, attaining a
maximum height of about three feet. Their texture was
like that of the white part of a cauliflower, though with
a tougher integument. In the damper grottoes, the
growths had more the appearance of our tree-agaricus,
and were often partially or wholly petrified. An altogether different type of vegetable growth hung down
from the ceilings of the drier caverns, in the form of
tangled and withered roots; which were, however, not
roots, but hollow stems of even diameter, about as thick
as a common pencil, divided into nodules or cells which
contained a kernel. As soon as they came across this
subterranean plant, the Green Child seized a section of
it, and breaking open its dry and flimsy sheath, offered
Olivero the kernels to eat. They were sweet and agreeable, and formed, the Green Child explained, the bread
of her people.

The first living thing they encountered was a bird, not
much bigger than a skylark, but more like an owl in appearance; for it was grey in colour, its downy feathers
like fur at a distance, and each eye was surrounded by
a ruff, or several rows of stiff concentric feathers. It differed from an owl, however, in having a straight beak;
and differed from any bird on earth in the manner of
its flight. Pointing its beak vertically upwards, it rose
as straight as a stone sinks, and when it had reached a
point about two-thirds the height of the grotto, gyrated
swiftly on its own axis. It descended in a corkscrew
motion and invariably took up its perch on a ledge about
six feet from the ground. Another peculiarity was that
it showed not the slightest sign of fear at the approach
of Olivero and the Green Child, and would, indeed,

freely allow itself to be touched and fondled. It was comparatively rare in distribution, and except during the mating season, solitary in its habits.

When they had traversed eight caverns, the Green Child suddenly stopped and laid a hand on Olivero's arm. They were near the entrance to a smaller grotto, an opening about the size of an ordinary doorway. As they listened, they heard a music of a distinct kind coming from within. Signalling Olivero to follow her, the Green Child went up to the entrance, and fell on her knees. Olivero did likewise, and then gazed upwards. He was looking into a grotto of small dimensions, perhaps twenty feet deep and thirty feet high. But it was a grotto of fairly regular proportions, rising in a conical formation, the walls a glittering mass of luminous crystals. At the back of the grotto was a human figure, a man with a high conical head, luminous green flesh like the Green Child's, and beard the colour of pale sea-weed. He was wearing a single diaphanous robe, and was seated on a low rock. Before him was a wide slab of rock, on which a few objects were standing. Most of these appeared to be polished crystals of various structure, some black like obsidian, some colourless like rock crystal. But the object which was engaging the attention of the inhabitant of the grotto was a miniature gong of the kind already described, consisting of a frame from which were suspended nine crystal rods. Each rod when struck emitted a different note, and the man before them was ringing the changes on this crystal carillon—that is to say, every time he struck the notes, he struck them in a different order, until all the possible orders were exhausted. On a carillon of nine notes, such a peal would not be complete until 362,880 changes had been rung.

Such cave-dwellers, the Green Child explained, were the wise men of her country, who lived in solitude engaged in these holy practices, and in the contemplation of polished stones.

After they had gazed at the cave-dweller for some minutes, they left him undisturbed, and continued their journey. From time to time they passed other grottoes, from which came the music of invisible bells, but they did not stop at any of these, but hastened onwards, guided by the chimes. After travelling for what seemed about six terrestrial hours, they came into a wide round space in which they saw a few figures moving about, carrying burdens. They emerged from grottoes on their right, proceeded across the hall and disappeared through an exit facing Olivero and the Green Child.

The chime conducted them round the walls of the great hall, past the grottoes on the right. Into one of these they ventured to look. It was thick as a forest with stalactites and stalagmites, but a wide pathway had been cleared down the middle, and on each side were blocks of stone which proved to be moulds, made of alabaster or steatite, into which the petrous moisture dripped. In some cases the influx was increased by moisture from the walls of the caverns, carried to the moulds in stone spouts.

In coming out of such a grotto, Olivero and the Green Child found themselves face to face with a group of five men. They were not dissimilar in appearance to the sage of the grotto; they wore the same diaphanous gown, their flesh was green, and they wore whitish wispy beards. They stared in goggle-eyed amazement at the two intruders, but made no sound or movement.

It was the Green Child who made the first approach. She had entirely forgotten the speech of her native country, but running up to the nearest of the group, she bared her arm and pointed to her green flesh, and then to his. She gesticulated excitedly, trying to indicate that she wished to accompany them. But they continued to stare at Olivero, who felt impelled to make some motion, some sign of friendly intention. But the moment he moved towards them, they started back in horror, as though they had been confronted with a ghost. And indeed, as such or worse than such, Olivero appeared to them; for actually the people of this country had no belief in disembodied spirits, and no knowledge of the different races of the world. In Olivero they suddenly saw a totally new species of human being; but only if you imagine a world in which there are no species, but only a single genus of mankind, can you get the measure of their surprise.

They fled precipitately; Olivero and the Green Child followed them leisurely, so as not to give the impression of pursuit. The cave through which they had disappeared was a short corridor leading into the vastest hall they had yet encountered; a large underground lake of space, perhaps three miles long and half as wide. Its ceiling was so high that its luminous expanse might have been taken for a sky by anyone not habituated to the solid structure of the earth. The light, however, was perfectly even, and continued without the variations of terrestrial light: an everlasting light, a summer evening fixed at the moment birds suddenly cease to sing.

The scene before them was too complex to be taken in at a single glance. The floor of the hall was a shallow oval basin, but the natural declivity of its sides had been interrupted by three wide terraces. The terraces were cut across by flights of steps, occurring at irregular intervals and apparently leading to the various exits—one such flight was at their feet. Above the terraces were many ledges, protruding at various levels, and on these ledges could be seen caves, either natural or perhaps hollowed out by human agency. The arena was even and unencumbered. To Olivero it seemed as though he were in the interior of an immense beehive or pigeon-cote.

The figures of the five men whom they had followed could be seen at the bottom of the steps, making straight across the arena at a running pace. They were approaching a dense group of people in the middle of the arena. Detached smaller groups could be distinguished on the three ledges.

The Green Child did not hesitate; and because he saw no other course, Olivero followed her down the steps, which were broad and long, and took about five minutes to descend. The floor of the hall, of greyish rock, was covered by an elaborate network of tunnels, designed to carry away excess moisture: they radiated towards the middle of the arena. There was no sign of any kind of vegetation, but occasionally a bird of the type they had already seen would rise gyrating in the air.

When they had advanced about half a mile, they were within hailing distance of the crowd they had seen from the top of the steps. The five men had disappeared into their mass. The crowd was standing perfectly still, facing the intruders.

Olivero and the Green Child halted when they came within fifty yards, but although they stayed still for a long time, nobody moved in the crowd, or gave any sign of their intention. They were like a flock of sheep watching the movements of some stranger, alert but uncertain what action to take. Olivero would have still waited, but the Green Child promised that there was no harm in her people; so, linking their arms together, they proceeded shyly forward.

They could now see that the crowd was composed entirely of young men and women, but the distinction between the sexes was not very evident, since all wore the same diaphanous robe, and on some of the youths a beard was not yet very obvious. All wore their blond hair long, and had unshod feet. Their bodies were excessively slender, their heads egg-shaped; they had no perceptible eyebrows, their eyes were tiny, but bright like a ferret's.

The nearest gave way before the approaching strangers, but turned when they had passed; there seemed to be about a hundred people in the group, and when Olivero and the Green Child went on, they all followed. It was then that Olivero noticed that they, too, walked in pairs, with arms interlinked.

Here and there on the plain other groups could be seen moving about, but the Green Child made for the middle point, perhaps guided by some obscure memory. At first the crowd followed in silence, but after a while they began to talk to each other in quick low voices.

In this manner they came to the middle of the plain, where there was a bubbling lake of warm water. The basin, which was perhaps two hundred feet across, had been made into a regular ellipse and was surrounded by a low wall, cut out of rock. Round the basin was an annular trough, some ten feet wide, of semi-circular section, and in this trough a number of naked men and women were bathing, all apparently of the same age as the crowd already encountered.

Seeing some of those accompanying them prepare to bathe, the Green Child divested herself of her terrestrial clothes and stepped into the basin. She was then in no way different from the other women there, except in age; and perhaps her flesh was of a slightly duskier shade of green. Olivero was now left feeling very incongruous in his black cloak and pantaloons, not to mention his shoes and other vestments. Many who were about continued to stare at him; so suppressing all feelings of shame or embarrassment, he threw off his cloak and other clothes and stepped with his white body into the chalybeate water.

It stung his flesh as from excessive saltiness, but presently the sensation became one of glowing warmth, which penetrated his whole flesh. He turned to where the Green Child reclined against the side of the trough; her head had fallen against her shoulder, and she seemed almost asleep.

If you go to sleep, he said, you might slip into the water and drown. He watched over her until he too began to feel overpowered by a desire to sleep. He therefore got out on to the ledge of the trough and pulled the Green Child after him. The rock there was warm, smooth as jade to the flesh. They lay there and sank into a profound slumber.

Since there was no measurement of time in this country, nor any consciousness of its passage, sensations could only be judged by their own intensity. Sleep which took all sensation away, took away the sense of duration. They might have slept there five minutes or five days or even five years; the same young people were about them when they awoke, but since these had never experienced a consciousness of time, none could tell them how long they had slept. Their terrestrial clothes had gone; at their feet they found each a diaphanous robe of the kind worn by the Green People.

In her sleep, perhaps because in such a state the mind

is accessible to influences which revive past memories, the Green Child had recovered her native speech. When she was fully conscious, she rose up crying *Si Siloën, Si Siloën*; which meant, I am Siloën. For that was her name before she was lost, and perhaps, when she was given the name of Sally on earth, it was because she had uttered this word often and Mrs. Hardie had hit upon the nearest English name known to her.

With the memory of her language, other memories had returned too, but only such as a child of ten or eleven would have. She remembered that certain of the wise men who dwelt in the caves governed the country and decided all matters in dispute. Turning then to the nearest inhabitants, she enquired for the cave of the wise men who governed. 'Many years ago,' she explained, 'I wandered away into the grottoes where there is no music and lost myself. Now I have returned with one who comes from another country, but was lost too, and now wishes to dwell among us."

Those to whom she spoke listened to her with grave innocent faces, and then pointed to a grotto beyond the third terrace, towards which a broad flight of steps led. When they had put on their robes, they climbed the steps and came to this grotto, which was like the others they had seen on their journey, though somewhat larger. Here, at equal intervals on five benches against the wall of the grotto, five bearded men were seated. The space before them was a bare space and into this stepped Siloën and Olivero.

The five figures did not move or betray any awareness of the interruption. But presently the one in the middle, seated opposite the entrance, spoke in a calm voice, and asked them what brought them into the presence of the Judges.

Siloën answered, and told them her strange story. Once or twice she stopped, as if to make sure that the mute immovable figures before her were actually listening, but on each occasion the Judge in the middle uttered one word, which meant: Proceed.

When she had come to an end of her story, Siloën was told to take Olivero with her and wait outside the cave until she heard a bell sounding within. So they went outside and sat there on a rock and looked down into the arena. They saw the same groups wandering about. On the three ledges were other groups, but progressively smaller. Those on the lowest ledge seemed to to be about fifty strong; those on the upper ledge only five strong. Other figures, sometimes in twos or threes, sometimes in stronger companies, moved up and down the flights of steps, disappearing occasionally into the mouths of the remoter caverns.

Whilst they waited outside the cave of the Judges, sitting together on a rock, they saw a group of five men approaching them along the upper ledge. They were dressed in the same uniform robe, their conical heads were bald except for a fringe of hair above the ears, their beards were whitish and wispy. The one in the middle, who was speaking, walked with head erect; the others looked downwards and meditated on what he said. When he came to the end of his discourse, he too adopted the meditative attitude, and the next of the group who wished to speak assumed the upright attitude. They paid no attention to anything about them, and passed Olivero and Siloën without a sign.

Presently from the cave came a sound like a xylophone being slowly struck. When Olivero and Siloën reappeared before the Judges, the one in the middle spoke again and told them to descend to the lowest ledge, and to stay there until they were satiated with the pleasures of youth; then they must separate and join with others who were passing into the second ledge, where they would enjoy the pleasures of manual work; and then, since his age already entitled him to pass beyond the second ledge, Olivero might proceed to the upper ledge, where he would enjoy the pleasures of opinion and argument. In that state he would stay a long time, until he was fit for the highest pleasure, which is solitary thought; and then he might retire to a distant grotto.

These instructions were delivered in an impassive voice, unaccompanied by any gestures. When it was evident that the Judge had no more to say to them, Olivero and Siloën retreated slowly, and descended the steps outside the grotto until they came to the lowest ledge. There they joined the first group they came across, and were accepted as companions without wonder or question.

Most of the time, the people within the group were paired off, male and female. They walked together, arm in arm, but with no appearance of excessively mutual devotion. Often, that is to say, when for any reason the group broke up into single units, they would reassemble in different pairs, without comment. The groups themselves were not rigidly constant; for when they descended into the arena, where they bathed and played games, the groups might become confused together, and on separating again, they would be composed of different units. There was no leadership within the group broke up into single units, they would reassemble limited to about fifty members.

They spent much time bathing, and in playing games which reminded Olivero of kiss-in-the-ring, rounders, and such like terrestrial games, in which many people could take part. The ledge was used as a promenade, and as a place for sleeping and copulating, both functions being performed with the same sense of naturalness. Since there was no measurement of time, they no doubt waited for the natural processes of their bodies to indicate the need for these functional acts; the one usually being the prelude to the other. But measured in terrestrial time, there is no knowing the frequency or the duration of these events. Time, it cannot be too often repeated, did not exist for these people.

When one of the maidens became pregnant, she left the group and lived in another large grotto, where she was attended by matrons. When she had given birth to a child, she returned to the group and did not leave the group until she was satiated with its pleasures, which happened when she had borne perhaps three children. But as the chances of conception were uncertain, and the period of gestation slow, this period was not necessarily short.

The Green Child at once assumed the habits and emotions of her people, but Olivero went through severe discipleship. He could take part with a good grace in all the games of these young people, but it was a long time before he could regard the pleasures of the flesh with the same innocence. He was angry and jealous when he saw Siloën walking arm in arm with one of the youths, and hid his convulsed face when he saw her making love with others. But gradually he grew ashamed of these terrestrial sentiments and finally they no longer disturbed him.

Olivero gradually learnt the simple language of these people; it was not difficult in itself, for it had no irregular inflexions and was devoid of abstract concepts. Its

difficulty consisted entirely of its unfamiliarity; it had
no Aryan roots, no relations with any language he had
known on earth; and it was entirely a spoken language.
This people had never conceived the idea of writing,
and no alphabet, no letters, no books of any kind existed
among them.

As was natural, Olivero exhausted the pleasures of the
third ledge much more quickly than Siloën, and by the
time he had learnt the language of the Green People,
and incidentally, was fully disintoxicated of all his
earthly sentiments, he was eager to proceed to the next
stage, and learn more of the customs of this strange
country. He therefore bade farewell to the group and
climbed the steps to the second ledge. He and Siloën
had already so merged themselves into the perfect
communion of the group, that it never occurred to
them to make any eccentric display of feeling on this
occasion.

Here Olivero had to wait until he found a gang (for
such the smaller groups on this ledge might be called)
with a vacancy caused by the promotion of a member
to the superior ledge; for on the second ledge, a much
stricter discipline prevailed, definite work being assumed
by each gang, and each gang proceeding from task to
task in a certain rotation. Olivero was lucky and fell in
with a gang of food-gatherers almost immediately.

It was an appropriate gang for a beginner, because
their task was the simplest of all. It was their duty to
search the caverns and grottoes for the earth-nuts and
fungi on which the inhabitants lived; to replenish the
stores of food which existed on each ledge; and to de-
liver rations to the solitary sages in their caves. In this
way Olivero became familiar with the immense range
of caverns and grottoes which constituted this under-

ground world. He never explored the farthest confines, because the gangs never went out of sound of the tinkling pendants, whose sound guided them through all the hollow intricacies. The fungi they collected in baskets woven from the dry roots of the earth-nuts; the earth-nuts were gathered with their pod-like stems complete, for when they had been shelled, the stems were not only used for making baskets, but their pulverised fibre was the raw material from which the diaphanous clothing worn by everybody was manufactured.

From the food-gatherers, after an indeterminate time, Olivero passed to the spinners and weavers. Their spindles were made of finely carved and polished crystal —a thin rod tapering towards each end, weighted in the middle with a disc of obsidian or chalcedony which served to give momentum and steadiness to the rotation. The fibres, having been separated in a stone mortar and pestle, were twisted into a thread, which was then attached to a notch at one end of the spindle. A rotatory motion was given to the spindle by twirling it between the thumb and fingers of the right hand, and then the fibres were drawn out in a fine uniform strand and so converted into yarn. Weaving was the simple interlacing of standard yarn, the woof being threaded by hand through a warp of about a hundred strands, fixed on a vertical frame of notched stone. The fabric made in this way was a loose gauze, silky in texture, but of broken surface.

Some of the occupations followed by Olivero were not of sufficient interest to be worth describing (works of irrigation, sanitation, stone-polishing and such like), but two of the higher grades of employment deserve mention. The first was the manufacture of gongs and crystals. It is perhaps not necessary to add anything to what has already been said of the gongs. They were made of innumerable sizes and of materials varying from fine needles of rock crystal to thick columns of stalactitic origin. The latter type were naturally rarer, on account of the long time required for their formation. The pendulums, as we might call them, when finished were passed on to another gang, whose business it was to arrange them in musical series—now a regular scale for ringing changes, now a number of notes which, striking against each other in succession, would make a recognisable melody.

The highest type of workman, however, was engaged on the polishing of crystals. For this purpose various kinds of rock were used—opal, chalcedony, fluorspar, limonite—but rock crystal was prized most on account of its purity. The science which we call crystallography —the study of the forms, properties and structure of crystals—was the most esteemed of all sciences in this subterrestrial country; indeed, it might be regarded as science itself, for on it were based, not only all notions of the structure of the universe, but equally all notions of beauty, truth and destiny. These questions occupied the sages on the uppermost ledge, and those who had retired like hermits to their solitary grottoes.

It is important to realise that the knowledge of crystals was of this formal nature, because upon it was built, like a superstructure, the whole concept of beauty. To put the matter briefly, their whole aim was to make crystals which, while retaining the apparent structure of each class, departed from the strict natural order in some subtle way. Æsthetic pleasure was a perception of the degree of transgression between the artificial form and its natural prototype, and the greatest æsthetic emotion was aroused by those crystals which transgressed most within the limits of probability. The six systems of crystal formation—the cubic, the tetragonal, the ortho-rhombic, the monoclinic, the triclinic and the hexagonal —were recognised, and each system had its devotees. Such preferences probably correspond to various phases of art in the terrestrial world—at one extreme the baroque fantasy of the cubic system, at the other extreme the classic simplicity of the hexagonal system.

The gangs whose duty it was to polish crystals began their careers by a prolonged study of natural crystals. Grottoes in which perfect specimens were ranged in series existed for easy reference, but an apprentice was not considered proficient until he had himself formed a collection of the complete series. This was not so easy as it might seem, for some of the classes were extremely rare, and it was necessary to search in the remote caves and grottoes beyond the zone of the musical guides.

When the education of an apprentice was complete, he was allowed to experiment on some of the less precious stones. The more he experimented, the more he became aware of the difficulty of his task; for there was no law but his own instinct to guide him beyond the limits of natural forms. But when once he had become sure of his instinct, then no joy could equal the discovery of a form whose perfection was other than the perfection of nature.

When he was satisfied that he had reached proficiency in the polishing of crystals made of opaque stones, the workman might then venture to use pure rock crystal. Though there was no actual control of the supply of this precious rock, it would have been regarded as a kind of blasphemy to employ the material for an imperfect work. When the workman was satisfied that he had succeeded in creating a perfect form, he might then test the result by offering the crystal to a solitary sage. If the sage accepted the gift for contemplation, then the work was judged perfect. When a workman had had five such crystals accepted, he was judged worthy of becoming a sage, and ascended to dwell on the uppermost ledge.

Many workmen were doomed to failure, either because their minds were too feeble to understand the laws of the natural world, or because, even granted that degree of intelligence, they were yet devoid of the instinct which can transgress the natural law in the interests of absolute beauty.

When they had admitted to themselves their failure, such workmen were invariably transferred to the other occupation which remains to be mentioned—the care of the caves of the dead.

It must now be explained that the people of this country had notions of immortality diametrically opposed to those prevalent on earth. Perhaps because instead of an open and impalpable sky they had solid rock above them; because they believed their universe to be limited in extent and human beings to be numerable—for whatever cause, they regarded the organic and vital elements of their bodies as disgusting and deplorable. Everything soft and labile filled them with a species of horror, and above all the human breath was the symptom of an original curse which could only be eradicated after death. Death itself was no horror to them, but nothing exceeded their dread of corruption and decay: that, to them, was a return to the soft and gaseous, to the very element of their weakness and disgrace. Their sole desire was to become solid—as solid and perdurable as the rocks about them. They therefore practised the rites of petrifaction. When the hated breath at last left the human body, that body was carried to special caves, and there laid in troughs filled with the petrous water that dripped from roof and walls. There it remained until the body turned white and hard, until the eyes were glazed under their vitreous lids, and the hair of the head became like crisp snail-shells, the beard like a few jagged icicles. But this process was merely a long purgatory, for when the body was finally petrified it was removed from its watery trough and carried like a recumbent statue to the halls of the dead—caves in which the alabaster bodies were stacked, one above the other in dense rows, to wait for their final beatitude, crystallisation. When the body, no longer recognisably human, but rather a pillar of salt, took on the mathematical precision and perfect structure of crystal, then it was judged to have attained its final immortality.

Slowly the caves were filling with these solid wedges. No man knew how far they extended into the infinite mass of the earth; all they knew was that the space they lived in was limited and that a time would come when the dwindling race would inhabit the last grotto, when the last of that race would plunge into the trough, and so fulfil the purpose of life, which is to attain everlasting perfection. For this people held that there was nothing else more acceptable unto God, than to offer their body wholly to the earth, and to unite it most inwardly with that earth. Then, they said, all their inward parts would rejoice, when their bodies were perfectly united with the earth. That was their whole desire: to be one with the physical harmony of the universe.

It will be easily imagined that the attendance on these petrifying grottoes and halls of the dead occupied the time of many men, but these duties never fell to Olivero, because he became so fascinated by the work of polishing crystals, and became so proficient in it, that before long he had qualified for the next stage of existence, one more appropriate to his age and experience. He therefore said good-bye to his fellow-workers, and climbing the steps, seated himself on a rock at the top.

The people walked there in groups of five, or singly. Those that walked singly had left a group to prepare themselves for the perfect solitude of a grotto; but to make the transition to such a state more gradual, they were permitted to circulate for so long as they could bear the sight of human beings on this upper ledge, and for last companions they were permitted to adopt a pet. Now the only living creatures in this underground world, except the birds already mentioned, were a species of blind-worm or snake, and an immense beetle, about the size of a tortoise. Usually speaking, a sage who liked beetles did not take to snakes, and *vice versa*; the respective characters of these two animals being rather similar to those of our dogs and cats. The snakes, which were about three feet long, were of a silver-grey colour, with faint gleams of phosphorescent blue in their scales. When domesticated (and it was rare to find one in a wild state) they would live about the person of their masters, for preference coiling round his neck, the head on his breast, the tail down his back. The beetles, on the other hand, did not make themselves familiar with the persons of their masters; they scuttled at their heels with the speed of cockroaches. Their shell-like wing-cases, of a blue metallic colour, were slightly striated in a longitudinal direction. They ran on three pairs of triple-jointed legs; their mandibles and antennæ were not conspicuous, but the females of the species (which did not greatly differ from the males in other respects) emitted a luminous glow from the hinder end of their bodies. They lived on dung, and were much esteemed as scavengers as well as companions.

It seemed an interminable time before Olivero saw a group approaching him which consisted of four men only. He rose when they were within speaking distance, and asked if he might join them. They bowed gravely, and made no objection; so Olivero took his place on the extreme left, for this was the position of the novice. As the leader of the group, who always occupied the middle position, departed to solitariness, so the novice would successively occupy the extreme right, the inner left and the inner right positions, until he himself finally became the leader.

It so happened that the group joined by Olivero was in the midst of a discussion of the notion of Time. This was not a problem that occupied the sages much, because in a country where there were no heavenly bodies, no succession of night and day, nor any variation of season, the sense of time was very rudimentary. It had never occurred to these people even to measure the passage of time, and they had no devices such as clocks and calendars. Nevertheless, they were sensible of change: the dripping of water in the grottoes, the trickling of streams, the ageing of the human body, and, above all, the process of petrifaction, were all phenomena which called for an explanation. Of one thing they all seemed convinced: that time was of limited duration. They pointed to the solidity and indestructibility of the rocks about them, and compared this mass, which to them was a more extensive element than space, with the insignificance of the things that change. When the last vital element had received its crystalline form, then the sense of time would disappear. Time is change, they said, and a mark of our transitional nature.

Olivero had been familiar on earth with the view that time is independent of experience, a pure form unaffected by all specific events; but this mode of reasoning was quite beyond their understanding. He ventured to suggest that the question should be judged from a standpoint wider than that of their present existence. We have no knowledge, he said, of the extent of the solid rock on every side of us; other worlds might exist hollowed out in its mass; and the solid universe itself might float in some wider hollow. In this wider universe there might be an endless process of change, and time, therefore, would be real and infinite.

But they laughed at his notion of a solid floating in space; it contradicted the law which makes all solid things fall through the air and sink in water. It was possible, they admitted, that other hollows existed in the universe, and they had to admit that the appearance of Olivero himself was a proof of this; but Olivero's description of the world he came from as one of boundless space was received as a wild fantasy; it was not possible, they held, to conceive of a space that was not bound in every direction by solids.

Olivero perceived that in his discussions he would have to moderate his sense of superior knowledge. Beyond a certain point, his experience would not be accepted. His evidence was of no more value than that of a man who had awoken from a vivid dream. His dream was real, but it was unique. It was not long before Olivero himself began to doubt the reality of his past. He longed to find Siloën again, to confirm his past impressions. But Siloën seemed to be for ever separated from him; and she herself, for that matter, was now firmly convinced that her whole earthly experience had been a nightmare, which had visited her whilst she lay exhausted and unconscious in the caves beyond the music.

When the leader of the group perceived how ignorant Olivero was of the basic principles of the universe, he asked leave of the other three to expound them briefly. The notion, he said, from which all our wisdom proceeds is that of Order in contrast to Disorder. He understood by Order not any abstract concept of an indeterminate kind, but the space-filling Mass about them. Disorder is empty space. Only Order exists; Disorder is not, and cannot be, conceived. From this fundamental idea they derived all their dogmas on the nature of the universe. Order cannot be imagined as having a beginning or an end; it cannot be created from Disorder or reduced to Disorder; for what is not Order, is not. Order is continuous throughout the universe, and is of one kind. It is indivisible, since it is everywhere the same, and there is nothing by which it could be divided. It is motionless and unchangeable, everywhere similar to itself. The world has no centre, but every centre within the world is a centre of Order. Thought itself is nothing other than Order; for it is thought of Order. Thought without Order is not thought, but nonsense. The senses are the cause of all Disorder, for being confined to the body, they create the illusion of self-hood. The only sensual perception which is true is that which shows us in everything an unchanging Order; other perceptions, as of the manifold variety of things, creation, destruction and change, tend to create a sense of Disorder, and are the cause of all error.

When Olivero, in acknowledging the force and perfection of this philosophy, ventured to suggest that the very concepts of Order and Disorder might be taken as the polar opposites that together constituted a single harmonious whole; and that this polarity might be the very principle of a universe constituted of space and emptiness, darkness and light, attraction and repulsion, life and death—when he put forward this view, which he did with difficulty for many of the images were meaningless to this people who, for example, lived in everlasting light and had no notion of darkness, they only laughed at him again, and said that it was the grossest of heresies to suppose the necessity of Disorder. Stopping the group in their slow peregrination, the leader turned outwards and pointed down into the wide basin of the grotto. A slight cloud of steam hung as usual above the warm waters of the spring; rose and drifted away in the soft currents of air that circulated through the caverns. Our life, he said, is like a cloud that rises from the earth; it floats in the air until it strikes the cooler surface of the rock, and there condenses, and becomes the more solid element of water. The water in its turn changes its form, solidifying on the surface of the rock. Everything solidifies : that is the law of the universe.

The expression used by these sages, meaning the law of the universe, was the nearest approach they had to our conception of God. Not knowing fire, not being subject to inclement seasons, not afflicted with thunder, lightning and all the terrors of the upper world, they had never evolved the instinct of fear. The universe to them was wholly passive, or only active in the gradual and inevitable establishment of order out of chaos. One people, without division of frontiers or language, they had no need to invoke supernatural aid. Neither sacrifice nor propitiation entered into their lives, because they had never endowed the law of the universe with personal attributes or human passions. Such a notion they would have regarded as the most outrageous blasphemy. It was only in their concept of beauty that they allowed for the exercise of an arbitrary will. Perhaps it is wrong to speak of beauty in this connection, for a system of æsthetics does not necessarily imply beauty in our sense. Their only fine arts were music and the construction of crystals. Music, as we have already seen, was merely a mathematical exercise—a ringing out of all the possible permutations on a given number of notes; and as such it was rather an exercise in the memory of order than what we should call an art. The contemplation of crystals was, however, a different matter; it was not a contemplation of all the possible systems of crystallisation (though this was one of their studies), but a sensual pleasure in the transgression of natural order. When eventually Olivero insisted on the discussion of this topic, the leader admitted that it was the most difficult problem in their philosophy. The only absolute beauty, the only beauty that was permanent and independent of temporal things, was the order of the universe as revealed in the structure of natural crystals. That was a truth admitted by everyone. But from the beginning of the world men had taken pleasure in making forms which were not exact imitations of the forms found in the rocks, but which were nevertheless suggested by these. The usual explanation given for such an extravagance was, that whilst the mind rejoiced in natural forms, the senses found pleasure in departing from these forms—not, it is true, to the extent of creating disorderly shapes, which would be a useless occupation; but sufficiently far to give them the pleasure which accompanies the discovery of an unknown order. Such orders outside nature did not really exist; but it amused men to imagine that they did.

Was it possible, Olivero asked, that the opposite explanation might be true: that actually it was the senses which, measuring things, rejoiced in the perception of the exact order of nature; and that it was the mind, asserting its liberty, which rejoiced in the forms created by man?

This question was discussed for many revolutions of the ledge (for that was the normal way of measuring the duration of their discussions); and was regarded as a bold paradox. It led them to an examination of the nature of the mind, and its relation to the senses: in the course of which they traversed many of the arguments long familiar to men of the upper world. The general truth, that the mind was fed by the senses and only formed by the process of sensual perception, was admitted. But just as the formless water which drips from the walls of a grotto turns into the perfect form of a crystal, so, they held, the incoming perceptions of the senses gradually formed an organ which had its own inherent sense of order. But this did not solve the problem posed by Olivero; for it was admitted that without a sense of order, there could be no perception of disorder.

They finally agreed to regard the forms of artificial crystals as belonging to an intermediate state, half-way between order and disorder. If this could be accepted as a reasonable hypothesis, then it was possible that some men, approaching the crystal from the side of the senses, saw in it an order created by the senses, and were pleased because such an experience gave them an illusion of human power sufficient to quell disorder; and that others, approaching the crystal from the side of the mind, were made aware of the distinction which exists between the order created by man and the order of the universe, and rejoiced in the superior nature of the order to which all flesh must eventually conform.

When this hypothesis had been made clear, and accepted by all the group, then Olivero suggested that those who approached the crystals from the side of the senses were those who actually made the crystals; whilst those who approached them from the side of the mind were the sages who accepted the crystals for contemplation.

To this proposition there was a general consent. Olivero from that moment advanced rapidly in the estimation of the group. He found it advisable to suppress his knowledge of another world and all his other worldly experience. But by keeping this knowledge to himself, regarding it as a secret store of dream imagery, he had a great advantage over his companions in their discussions. They all marvelled at his eloquence and wisdom, but Olivero was not aware of any special effort on his part; for though thoughts were subtle in this country, lives were simple; and a certain complexity of experience is essential to eloquence. For the rest, his curiosity was sufficient to provide continual scope for argument and enquiry.

One by one the positions in the group were resigned to him, until he was finally elected leader. In that condition he might well have remained until his death, for he found it very pleasant to circle round that even ledge, in the steady luminous atmosphere of the grotto. Such food as they required—and it was infinitesimal by the standards of the outer world—was waiting for them in baskets placed at intervals along the path. Water for drinking was found in stoups cut out in the surface of the rock. The temperature, now that Olivero was acclimatised, was agreeable and constant. Illness,

THE GREEN CHILD

even the least irregularities of health, was completely
unknown. Age came to the living body like petrifaction
to the dead body—an infinitely slow process; and the
nearer the body approached to death, the more beautiful appeared the state of solid and crystalline perfection. When, very old by our standards, they finally
died, the event was peaceful. Going on their rounds to
the solitary sages, the food-gatherers would at rare intervals find a figure sitting rigid and silent in its grotto,
his hand no longer ringing changes on the bells. Com-
petently, without emotion, they would lay out the body
of the sage, placing his favourite crystal on his breast.
Then they would inform the attendants on the caves of
the dead, who went and fetched the body and brought
it to the petrifying-trough. So indifferent were these
people to death, that if such a procession passed a band
of youths and maidens playing, or a gang of workers
or even a group of sages in disputation, these went on
with their occupations: no more attention was paid to
the dead than if a breeze had passed, shaking notes
from the hanging bells.

The time came when Olivero felt that he should seek
the solitary state, and his mind being fully made up,
he announced his intention to the group. They accepted
his decision without demur, for it was not usual to
question the wisdom of a group leader. The only rule
of the community was that a sage seeking solitude
should first present himself to the five judges, not that
his decision should be questioned, but to give the leading judge himself an opportunity to retire. If he availed
himself of this opportunity, then the aspirant took the
place on the left of the judges, and resigned himself to
another cycle of promotion, one which might endure
much longer than the one he had just passed through.

But actually the post of judge was not often vacated; for though no special privileges attached to it, and though rarely called upon to function, nevertheless a special grace inhered in the notion of authority, one which appealed strongly to a certain type of sage.

There was no thought of retaining Olivero, so he left the cave of the judges feeling elated. He had now reached the final stage of life, when nothing would be of any concern to him but the freedom of his own mind. He would willingly have dispensed with the solitary promenades with a pet; but when he made such a proposal to the judges, the leader strongly advised him not to omit a ritual which had so much sound sense behind it; for it was not merely a question of slowly dissociating oneself from the community of men, but by living for a time in the company of an insect or a reptile, creatures unable to communicate their thoughts, the mind was prepared for the process of communicating with inanimate things. For though these sages sought solitariness, they were well aware of the dangers of introspection, and therefore trained themselves to direct their thoughts to an object outside themselves. Without an object to contemplate, they would say, the eyes roll inwards, and we become blind. This object, by an ageless convention, was always a crystal.

Olivero therefore went in search of a beetle, for he preferred their hard precise form to the sinuous and sly snake. Young beetles awaiting a master were kept in a special grotto, to which a sage might repair and make his choice. There was little difference between any of them, except in the matter of size, but Olivero selected one which, from the way it waved its mandibles, he judged to be of a lively disposition. For Olivero, in spite of his acclimatisation, was still more vigorous and muscular than the other inhabitants, and apt to walk more briskly than was usual. He therefore wanted a beetle that could run quickly, and keep up with him.

Cypher, as he called his beetle, was an ideal pet. If Olivero stopped to rest, Cypher moved to the side of the track, and from an inconspicuous spot watched his master. His mandibles and antennæ might move playfully, but never for a second did his eyes, which protruded like black glassy beads, shift their gaze, and the moment Olivero rose, the beetle moved intelligently into the middle of the path, ready to speed along at his master's heels. Olivero was touched by such efficient devotion, and although he felt no temptation to lavish human sympathy on the beast, yet he found him pleasant to talk at—lively but dumb, patient but ever eager to advance, never showing any symptoms of tiredness, boredom or dislike.

It is impossible to say how long Olivero continued in this state, but certainly he found it more enjoyable and therefore more necessary than he had anticipated. But finally he had become so accustomed to exteriorising his thoughts in the direction of Cypher, that he felt he could safely trust himself with the inanimate world, and that he should delay no longer to seek his grotto. He therefore took Cypher for a last walk, and left him in the care of certain workers, who tended discarded pets. Such pets were not given to strange masters, but were kept in special caves where with females of the species they propagated their kind.

The manner in which it was customary to seek a grotto for final retirement was this: The sage perambulated slowly round the upper ledge. As he came to every cavern that led off from the central grotto, he listened to the particular music of that cavern, and there were perhaps sixty of them. When he had traversed the whole ledge in this way, he would repeat the performance, until he could carry the individual melodies of the caverns in his mind, and from among them he would finally select that which pleased him best. Then he would set off down this cavern, and wherever he came to a crossing, again he would make a choice, and follow whither his ear dictated. As he went along, he would glance into the grottoes he passed, and at any point on his journey he might make his choice of an empty grotto. But naturally the best grottoes within near reach of the central grotto would be occupied, and unless he came across one recently vacated by a dead sage, he might have to wander a considerable distance. If in this process he came to a place where the music ceased, then he must wait in that place until the food-gatherers came, and from that point take them with him. His choice finally made, the food-gatherers returned and instructed the bell-makers to prepare gongs of the particular chime followed by the sage, which were afterwards fixed as a guide for future food-gatherers.

After twice circling the ledge, Olivero selected a cavern whose bells gave out a melody in the Lydian mode. For a long time he had stood at the entrance of this cavern, listening to the soft notes carried on the sweet air that swept gently along the passage. Like most of the melodies, it consisted of only seven notes, but notes so delicately poised, so subtly modulated, that they carried in their pitch and intervals the sublimest sense of intellectual beauty. There could be no further hesitation, but Olivero indulged in that intensest pleasure which is ours when we prolong that last instant of indecision, already aware of the joy awaiting us, but anxious to observe it before making it irrevocably ours. For when a pleasure such as this is made habitual, it loses in acuteness what it gains in accumulation and depth.

Olivero, in those moments, wondered what kind of being he was who invented the melody, but there was no knowing since melodies sufficient for all the caverns had been composed by sages long ago, and were venerated as intellectual heirlooms. It is possible, of course, that sages of his own time might be capable of composing melodies as beautiful, but no value was attached to change in itself; a thing once beautiful, it was thought, was always beautiful, and the work of art was created only out of necessity.

When he had indulged this mood of sensuous anticipation, Olivero began his last journey. For some way, enraptured by the music, he did not think to look into the grottoes he passed. When finally he recollected his mission, he had gone far, and found the first grotto he entered vacant. It must have been occupied on some previous occasion, for the seat of rock and the rock slab in front of the seat were already prepared. It was a grotto of medium size, oval in section, conical in elevation. Its walls were of a darker basic rock than any Olivero had previously seen, a luminous obsidian, very perfect in its crystalline formation. It was free from stalactites, and from all trace of moisture; the entrance, being high and wide, provided sufficient means of ventilation.

Olivero stood at the threshold, still and intent for a long time. The space of the grotto was growing round him, becoming real in all directions. Before committing himself to dwell for the rest of his mortal life in this room, he wished to test its confines, to make sure that its shape would continue to please him. He found it

fully pleasing; the walls arched upwards shallowly con-
cave until they reached the high apex, which was
round and deep, glistening and bluish, like the freshly
exposed socket of a bone. To gaze upwards was like
gazing into the iris of an immense illuminated eye.

Olivero went over to the rocky bench, and seated
himself facing the entrance. Against the even glow of
the rock surface the aperture was hardly visible. It was,
however, the direction from which he could still hear
the chime of the bells.

He now waited in that timeless atmosphere, very still,
scarcely varying his posture. His body at first felt the
strain: the complete inactivity, the pressure of the hard
rock. But the mind coaxed the body into endurance,
into final contentment.

The food-gatherers found him eventually, and
brought him supplies of food and water. One day they
brought him a chime of nine bells, and a rod to strike
them. It was exquisitely tuned, and Olivero found great
pleasure in ringing the changes. To ring a full peal
would take as long as fourteen days, judged by terrestrial time; but now Olivero had lost all consciousness
of terrestrial time, and judged all things by their inherent duration.

Occasionally he was disturbed by crystal-cutters, who
came with crystals to offer him. But the crystal he desired was one which echoed in its proportions the
melody of the music outside his grotto. That is to say,
it should consist of seven planes without symmetry, but
with axes meeting in a single point. Though he accepted
other crystals which pleased him by their natural and
absolute beauty, he reserved the place of honour in the
middle of his slab for a crystal that should have the
particular harmony of the music that had brought him

to this place. It was only because the crystal-makers perceived in what direction his preference lay, that finally they produced a crystal having these properties. It was of large size, ten inches high, light entering and emerging from its polished surfaces in a manner which produced a series of vivid colours, varying between pale gold and steely blue.

Olivero now had all that he required for the life of contemplation, and for the preparation of his body for the perfection of death. When not lost in the ecstasy of objective proportions, crystals and bells, he found the greatest pleasure in anticipating the objectivity of death. He looked forward to that time when the body is released from the soul, and the soul from the body, and the body exists in itself. He had acquired that final wisdom, which sees in the soul a disturber of the peace of the body. The soul it is that incites the senses to seek spiritual satisfactions. But the only satisfactions are physical, measured and immutable. The body knows no real bliss until it has gathered into itself the wavering antennæ of sight and hearing, when nothing from the outer world troubles its inner perfection, when it has no sense or desire, but aspires after fixed and harmonious being. All absolute things, absolute beauty and absolute good, and the essence or true nature of everything, these are not apprehended by the fickle senses, but achieved by the body itself when it casts off the worm that has devoured it and filled it with itches and desires, and takes on a state of crystalline purity. Purest knowledge itself is not a shifting process of perception, but a final state of existence. Nothing can exist finally but matter, and nothing can exist eternally but matter in harmonious form. What is chaos but matter disturbed by immaterial forces?

When Olivero considered all these things, he was led to reflect in this manner: Have I not found a path of action which brings me to the conclusion, that while we are alive, and the body is infected by the soul, our desires are never satisfied? For the soul is a source of endless trouble to us by reason of its lust for power; and is liable also to diseases which overtake us and impede us in the search for true existence: it fills us full of loves, and lusts, and fears, and fancies of all kinds, and of pride; indeed, it often takes away from us the very capacity of action. When it moves us to action, then often as not the action is destructive of the body. Whence come wars and rebellions? whence but from the spirit and the lusts of the spirit? Wars are occasioned by the love of power and power has to be acquired by force to satisfy the demands of spiritual pride. By reason of all these incitements and disturbances, we have no time in life to give to philosophy. Even if we find a moment's leisure, and give ourselves to some speculation, the soul is always breaking in upon us, causing turmoil and confusion in our enquiries, and so amazing us that we are prevented from seeing the truth. Experience has proved to me, that if we would have pure knowledge of anything we must be quit of the soul—the body in itself must achieve a state of harmony and perfection. Then we attain the absolute beauty that we desire, and of which we say that we are lovers; not while we live, but after death. For then, and not till then, the body will be parted from the soul, and exist in itself alone. In this present life, we make the nearest approach to perfection when we have the least possible intercourse or communion with the soul, and are not surfeited with the spiritual nature, but keep ourselves pure until the hour when God is pleased to release us. And thus having got rid of the fluctuations of the spirit, we shall be pure and become part of the universal harmony, and know in ourselves the law of the physical universe, which is no other than the law of truth. When my body shall have acquired this final harmony, then I know that I shall have come to the end of my journey, and attained that which has been the pursuit of my life. All that is misty and fluid, all that is soft and labile, falls, precipitates, returns to the chaos of unformed matter; but out of the same chaos is slowly formed all that is finite and solid, all that is hard and eternal, all that is fixed and harmonious. This harmony exists before life and after life; in worlds that are not yet formed and in worlds that are defunct, cold and extinct. Such harmony is the harmony of the universe as well as the harmony of the crystal; my only desire is to become a part of that harmony, obeying in my frame its immutable laws and proportions.

When death came to Olivero, he felt with peculiar joy the gradual release of his limbs from the streams of blood and the agents of pain that had for so long kept possession. He died slowly, and calmly watched the pallor spreading, the marmoreal stiffness gripping the loose flesh, locking joints and ventricles. The beating of his heart was like the jumping of a flame in an empty lamp. Summoning his last vital effort, he stifled for all time that anxious agitation.

The attendants on the caves of the dead who carried his body to the petrifying-trough met on their way another procession, coming from the grottoes where the matrons lived. These were carrying the body of Siloën, who had died at the same time. The two bodies were laid side by side in the same trough, and these two who had been separated in life grew together in death, and became part of the same crystal harmony. The tresses of Siloën's hair, floating in the liquid in which they were immersed, spread like a tracery of stone across Olivero's breast, twined inextricably in the coral intricacy of his beard.

THE END